Their Last Hope

Sarah Ettritch

NORN PUBLISHING
TORONTO, CANADA

CHAPTER ONE

L IZ PRICE STRODE to her office, ignoring those who caught her eye and pretending she hadn't heard anyone who spoke to her. The speech she'd give at a fundraiser tomorrow night sat on her desk, ready to be reviewed. Determined to focus, to take her mind off the cancer eating away her life and be productive until the last second, damn it, she dropped into her chair and grabbed the printed sheets. She preferred to review a hard copy. Mistakes she'd missed on the screen jumped out at her.

A minute later, she reached for a pen. She'd written *With your continued support, I am absolutely confident that we will see sentient machines in my lifetime.* She drew a line through "in my lifetime." She could say it. Those listening to her wouldn't have a clue. But she'd know.

Artificial Intelligence Today had profiled her last month and breathlessly predicted that her contributions to the field would be key to bringing androids to life. But she wouldn't be there when the first android became self-aware. She'd be rotting away, her life cut short at thirty-eight.

When she'd received her diagnosis that morning, her doctor had recommended that she resign her research position and go on a holiday. She'd nodded, even though she'd had no intention of following his advice. She'd squeeze every last minute out of this useless body, spend as much time as she could at the AI Centre. She wouldn't waste the last months of her life lying around on a fucking beach.

Resentment surged through her, and she tossed the pen aside. She'd rather be in the lab tomorrow night, not begging for coin. Time was of the essence now. Fundraisers were boring. She'd have to freeze a smile on her face and speak with—

A conversation she'd had with a billionaire at a fundraiser a few months ago came back to her. She hadn't given it any thought at the time, but now . . . Maybe she wouldn't rot away, after all.

"FROZEN?" MOM DABBED at her eyes with a tissue. "Why would you want to do that?"

Sitting in an armchair across the living room from Mom, Liz sipped her water. She wanted wine, but it wouldn't mix well with her medication. "Because it will give me a chance to live again."

"Do you really think they'll be able to unfreeze you and you'll be . . ." Mom searched for the right words. "All right? You'll be you?"

"Yes, I do. Science marches on. Look at what we know now that we didn't know a hundred years ago."

"I think it's morbid. How will it work? When you pass away, won't you want to be with your father? He's in heaven now. He's waiting for us." Mom's brow furrowed. "Or do you go to heaven and then come back?"

"I haven't really thought about it." Nor did she care. "I'm sure God can accommodate cryonics," she said, for Mom's benefit.

"But does he want to? And how much will it cost? It must be expensive. You'll have to be stored somewhere." Mom's face crumpled. She snapped another tissue from the box on the coffee table. "I don't think I can talk about this."

Liz leaned forward. "I need you to. I don't have much time. If I suddenly collapse, you'll have to call the cryonics group. They recommend moving to a medical facility near the cryonics centre, but my research is here, and I don't want Nic to have to change schools."

Mom shredded the tissue she held and let the pieces fall to the coffee table. "Have you told her?"

"Not yet." How would she explain it to a seven-year-old? God, she really wanted that wine. "She's young. She'll get over it."

"For god's sake, Liz, you're her mother." Mom's voice dropped. "It doesn't matter that you hardly pay any attention to her. She'll still be devastated."

"She'll adapt."

Mom gaped at her.

"I'll tell her tom—" Nic's high-pitched voice made Liz break off.

Nic breezed into the living room. "I'm here to say night-night." She threw herself at her grandmother. "Night, Nana."

Mom held her tight. "Good night, Nic. Don't let the bed bugs bite."

Nic's face scrunched up. "Ew." She crossed the room and stood in front of Liz. "Night, Mommy."

Liz set her water down and gave Nic a quick hug. "Good night. Now, off you go."

Nic padded away, her footsteps fading away as she climbed the stairs. Silence settled over the living room. Liz sipped her water again. Mom was staring at her. Irritated, Liz looked away, but grief suddenly tightened her throat. She wasn't the greatest mother or daughter, but she loved them.

"How much is this freezing thing going to cost?" Mom finally said. "I bet it's in the thousands—the hundreds of thousands."

Liz turned back to her. "That's why I'm glad I have life insurance. All I have to do is change the beneficiary to the cryonics centre."

"What about Nic?"

"I have savings, and I started contributing to an education fund the moment she was born. I haven't completely failed at my maternal duties."

"She needs more than your money. She's always needed more than your money." Mom's eyes lit up. "Why don't you cash in that insurance policy and hand in your notice at work? Pull her out of school for a month. Spend time with her. Go on a holiday. Take her to Disney World."

"I don't want her falling behind in school." Plus, it would be cruel. What would be the point of trying to forge a closer relationship with Nic when Liz would kick the bucket soon afterward?

She hadn't been cut out to be a mother, but she'd never

regretted not having an abortion. She'd considered it, but the thought of terminating her own flesh and blood had felt cold. The irony of caring more about the embryo in her womb than the child upstairs wasn't lost on her. Mom had once said that she cared more about her androids than she did about Nic. Maybe she was right. Fortunately Nic had a grandmother who loved her to bits.

"About Nic, Mom." A lump rose in Liz's throat. She looked down at her lap and blinked back tears. Damn, she hadn't expected this. "Will you take—I mean . . ." She lifted her head.

Mom's eyes glistened. "Of course I will."

"You'll get everything except the life insurance."

"I don't care about the money."

"Use it. Take Nic to Disney World."

Mom's expression said it all. *Yes, Mom, I know.* But she wouldn't. With the help of her assistants, she might squeeze out one last paper, or at least get far enough that Duncan could finish one for her and not begrudge naming her as one of the paper's authors.

"I still can't believe it," Mom said, her eyes welling again. "Do you feel sick?"

"I'm up and down. According to the doctor, it won't be long before I'm down most of the time."

Mom flinched, but Liz wouldn't sugar-coat anything for her. With everyone else, yes, but not with Mom, who'd always faced life head on. "I'll give you the contact information for the cryonics centre. The moment it looks like I'm on the way out, you have to call them. They have to be there when

I die, otherwise it will be too late to preserve me." It was all about saving the brain. No point reviving her if she were a vegetable.

"To think we thought it might be a food allergy."

Mom had thought so. Liz had expected to see her doctor, get a prescription for something trivial, and feel wonderful again next week. When the doctor had sent her for tests, and then more tests, she'd thought he was being thorough, and perhaps overly cautious. He'd mentioned cancer, but among a list of other possibilities. *Fuck cancer. Fuck it to hell.*

She spent the next hour answering Mom's questions, alternating between giving her information and reassuring her that she wouldn't drop dead that night. "I'm tired, Mom," she said around nine.

Mom's eyes widened.

Liz's jaw tightened. "Don't do that."

"What?"

"Treat me like I'm sick and frail. I'm just tired. It's been a rough day."

"Do you want me to come over tomorrow and cook dinner?"

"No. Well, you can, but only Nic will be here. I have a fundraiser." She ignored Mom's frown and stood, hoping Mom would follow her lead. They normally didn't hug at the door, but when Mom reached for her, Liz didn't protest. "Will you be okay?" she murmured into Mom's ear.

"I should be asking you that." Mom drew back. "I have room for both of you . . . when you need it."

"I'd rather you come here, so Nic is at home."

"I'll come here, then." Mom pulled her into another hug and squeezed her. "You know you can call me any time, day or night."

Liz patted her back. "I know."

After seeing Mom out, she put their dirty glasses into the dishwasher and went upstairs. On her way to the bathroom, she quietly opened Nic's bedroom door and peered inside. Nic was fast asleep, her right hand tucked under her pillow. According to Mom, Nic had Liz's eyes and chin. She also had her mind. Nic was bright and curious and doing well in school. Liz couldn't help but smile. Their longest conversations were about Mommy's work, and Nic always asked thoughtful questions. What would she be like when she grew up? Would she think about her mother? Would she follow in her mother's footsteps? She had a silly side that must have come from her father. Nic was capable of having fun for the sake of having fun, something Liz had always found a waste of time. But Nic was smart. Liz was sure she'd make something of herself.

You'll be fine, Nic. You'll be fine without me. You always have been. I'm sorry. You deserved better. Liz pulled the door shut, then pressed her forehead against it and closed her eyes.

LIZ FINISHED TYPING a sentence for the paper she would pass to Duncan, then leaned back in her chair and closed her eyes. Lifting her arms and moving her fingers took so much energy. Her nausea had worsened, and her pain now laughed at any pills she popped. Everyone who dared talk to her about her condition was urging her to leave her office for good. Her oncologist had brought up palliative care. Nobody understood that she had to push on, get all her ideas and predictions and insights down on virtual paper. She couldn't stand the thought of them dying with her. Although she wouldn't admit it to her, she agreed with Mom. Cryonics was still in its infancy. Having herself frozen would give her a chance at cheating death, but only a small one.

At least her death would contribute to science. The medical personnel who'd try to revive those in an icy slumber would fail before they succeeded, but they'd learn from each failure. Maybe she'd be one of the first to open her eyes in a new age, and with a fully functioning brain.

Someone tapped on her open office door. She took a second to open her eyes. Tyler, one of her students, hovered in the doorway. She motioned for him to come inside.

"Are you all right?" he asked.

"I'm fine," she said, surprised at how weak her voice sounded. Had that just happened, or had she only just noticed? "What do you want?"

He shifted his weight. "I know you've arranged for me to work with Dr. Nassar, but I've decided to transfer to another department."

Shock stabbed through her. Tyler was one of her brightest students. She'd expected him to carry on her work and become a familiar name in AI journals. "Why?"

"I just—I've come to realize this isn't what I want to do with my life. To be honest, I've been wrestling with this for a while."

"Why? Where are you going?"

He smiled sheepishly. "I know this might sound crazy, but

the more I've studied here, the more I've become impressed with us, our physiology. I'm switching to neuroscience."

"You're not serious."

"I didn't decide this on a whim. It's been a while, and then when I heard . . . when you . . ."

"It's okay, Tyler. Just say it."

He slowly exhaled. "When I heard about your cancer and that, well, it's terminal, it made me think about my own life."

Great, she'd become the dying schmuck who made everyone else face their own mortality, thank some deity they weren't her, and do what they hadn't had the courage to do before. She was so happy she could be of service.

"I figured since I have to change supervisors, it would be a good time to make the break," Tyler said.

She folded her arms and leaned back in her chair, making it squeak. "I don't understand it, but it's your life."

"I couldn't stop thinking about the end game."

"What do you mean?"

"Where will all this lead? What are we trying to do? Machines are already putting people out of work, and it's only going to get worse. Why are we trying to create machines that will eventually be more intelligent than we are?"

She wanted to roll her eyes, but she didn't have the energy. "Will it hurt your ego?"

"No, I'm afraid it'll get us all killed."

A wave of nausea prevented her from replying. She needed to put her head down for a few minutes.

"I've also been having doubts about machines gaining consciousness," Tyler continued. "Our algorithms, our instructions, will always be at the root of it. So what if a machine can beat someone at chess or compose a new song and play it perfectly? I can guarantee you it wouldn't have been up all night worrying about its performance, or feeling like it has to throw up just before it went on stage."

"And you see that as a bad thing?" Liz managed to say, wishing he hadn't mentioned throwing up.

"I wouldn't see it as an accomplishment. A sentient machine will be a wind-up toy or a mindless puppet, dancing to an algorithmic tune." Tyler mimicked the movement of a puppet on a string, then tapped his right temple. "I've come to appreciate that we've got a damn good computer up here. And there's still so much we don't understand about it. Let's understand ourselves before we create something we won't be able to control."

She'd never pegged Tyler as someone afraid to break new ground. He probably thought there should be no space travel until they'd solved all their problems on this planet, too. She couldn't disagree with him more, especially now, when she was almost out of runway. What was the point of this damn good computer inside her skull when everything it learned, and all the new neural pathways it laid down, were ultimately snuffed out? If she could download her consciousness into a machine and get rid of this frail biological water bag, she would. If there was a way to eliminate all the bullshit like fear and guilt, she'd be the first in line.

Machines *would* surpass humans. She wished she could be around to see it. Maybe she would be. In its present state, cryonics was a long shot, but hell, it was a chance. As for Tyler, it sounded like he'd never belonged here at the centre.

She forced a smile. "I hope it works out for you."

"Thanks."

Wanting what could be his last conversation with her to end on a strong note, she slowly rose, rounded her desk, and stuck out her hand. "Thank you for—" Her right knee buckled. Her reflexes didn't kick in. She hit the floor—hard. Pain lanced through her right shoulder.

"Liz?"

She tried to push herself up, but her arms wouldn't obey her. Tyler's face swam into view.

"Liz?"

She opened her mouth. Nothing came out.

"Shit!" Tyler disappeared. Scrabbling, then: "Yes, I need an ambulance at the Martin Goodkind Research Centre, fourth floor. My supervisor just collapsed . . . Yes, she's breathing . . . No, she can't talk. She has—"

Darkness.

LIZ SUCKED AIR into her lungs, then gathered her strength for her next breath. Why was she fighting? It was over. They weren't going to rush in and tell her they'd found a cure.

Mom leaned over and brought the straw sitting in water to Liz's lips. Liz kept her lips closed and caught Mom's dismay before she masked it.

"The cryotics? Crygenics? The team is here," Mom said. "They're ready."

Good. Her eyes slid shut. A door opened. "How's she doing?" someone—Liz thought it was the short nurse who chattered away when she checked her vitals—murmured.

"She's hanging in," Mom said, a tremor in her voice.

"I'll check in again in about fifteen minutes," the nurse said.

Fifteen minutes? Was that all she had left? Fifteen fucking minutes?

The door closed. Mom's fingers grasped Liz's. Her hand felt warm, comforting. "Nic's with Donna," Mom said, referring to the friend she'd known for over fifty years. "She wanted to come with me, but I said you didn't want her to see you this sick. You didn't want her to remember her mother like that, and she didn't want to remember you like that."

If Liz could speak, she'd thank Mom for following her wishes.

"Maybe she should have come, though. She wanted to be with you. She loves you."

It's too late for me to become a wonderful mother now, Mom. And if you haven't noticed, I'm dying, here. Give it a rest. She knew Mom didn't mean to criticize. She was thinking of Nic, who may have lost out on the mother lottery, but had hit the jackpot when it came to grandmothers. Liz was grateful. She wasn't lying here wondering who would take care of Nic, who would love her and nurture her and encourage her to grow up to be her own woman.

She took another laboured breath. Each one was harder now. Ten minutes? Five? She'd been born too early, when they were on the cusp of so many medical breakthroughs. A few weeks ago, she'd seen a report about how researchers may have identified cancer's Achilles' heel, and another one about training the immune system to obliterate cancer cells. It wouldn't do her any good, not until she was unfrozen. If only she'd been born later, or this damn cancer had waited until she was older. Liz was certain she would have been able to download her consciousness into some gadget, or have her organs replaced with synthetic ones. But unfortunately she'd be in the group that others would look back on and think, "Poor bastards, they only lived a short while and then poof, they were gone," just as she'd looked back in pity at those who'd lived when making it to thirty was an accomplishment.

Another breath . . .

"Can I go on that ride, Mommy?"

Liz looked down at Nic. "What?"

Nic pointed at the merry-go-round. "That ride?"

She let go of Nic's hand, picked her up, and kissed her forehead. "Of course you can."

"What?" Mom's fingers tightened. "What are you trying to say?"

Liz braked when she heard the crash behind her. She leaped off her bike and let it fall to the ground. A piercing wail set her heart racing. She ran to Nic, chiding herself for riding ahead of her. She should have had Nic ride in front.

Nic sat on the road, clutching her right leg. Tears streamed down her cheeks.

"Are you okay?" Liz crouched next to her and studied the raw, angry wound on Nic's right knee. "I know it hurts, but it's just a scratch. We'll need to clean it and put a Band-Aid on it, but you'll be okay," she said soothingly.

Nic's tears still flowed.

Liz smiled at her. "Why don't we go home and take care of you, hmm? You can choose which Band-Aid we put on, okay?"

Tears turned to sniffles.

"We'll have some chocolate ice cream, too," Liz said.

Nic let go of her leg. "Do we have sprinkles?"

"I believe we do." Liz took Nic's hand and helped her to her feet. They peered at Nic's bike. "It survived," she said lightly. "No harm done."

"I'm sorry, Mommy."

"Don't be sorry. It happens to all of us." She picked up the bike and waited for Nic to mount it, but Nic gazed up at her. "What is it?" Liz asked.

Nic reached for her. Liz carefully set Nic's bike down and hugged her. "You'll be okay."

"I'm not hugging you for me, Mommy. I'm hugging you for you."

"Why?"

"Because I love you."

A lump rose in her throat. "I love you, too. I love you more than you'll ever know."

Her heart stopped.

CHAPTER TWO

S HE OPENED HER eyes to blinding glare. Her eyes reflexively closed.

"It's too bright," someone said. "Dim the light." Rustling, then, "Can you hear me? Hello? Can you hear me?"

Elizabeth Price. Liz. That was her name.

"Can you hear me?"

"Shit. I knew this wasn't going to work." Another voice. Deeper.

"How much time do we have?"

She cracked her left eye open. Two men hovered over her, one with a bushy black beard, the other clean-shaven.

"I'm surprised they haven't noticed yet. We could have minutes, seconds . . ." A woman, sounding far away.

"They might not care," the clean-shaven man said. "They haven't taken anyone stored here."

"I thought you said you could bring her around in under five." The woman again.

"After she was thawed and revitalized," he snapped.

"She's been revitalized for almost twenty minutes."

"One of her eyes is open," the bearded man said.

The other man's brows shot up, then he grinned. "Good, we're in business. Can you hear me?"

"Yes," Liz croaked. Her throat was on fire.

"Excellent. Sit up for me, will you?"

Before she had a chance to respond, he grabbed her hand and pulled. She popped into a sitting position. The room spun. "My head," she groaned, grabbing it.

He frowned and looked at the bearded man. "We're going to have to carry her out."

"The best laid plans," the bearded man muttered. "If you can haul her, I'll keep them off us."

The other man nodded and peered at Liz. "Do you know your name?"

She swallowed, trying to moisten her throat. "It's—"

"Alarm!" the woman shouted.

Alarm? Liz didn't hear anything.

"We've got to move. Now! Pick her up, Tony."

Liz's stomach roiled when the clean-shaven man—Tony—threw her over his shoulder like a sack of potatoes. Her arms dangled helplessly down his back. Using all her strength, she managed to lift her head, and glimpsed a steel table, cupboards, used syringes and their wrappers on the tiled floor, a wheeled table next to the steel one. Then the room receded. A woman briefly swung into view; she was peering at a gadget in her hands. "Come on," she said, and was gone.

They rushed down a sterile corridor. Liz lowered her head and closed her eyes. If Tony's strides hadn't been jolting her, she would have nodded off.

"Right now, they're behind us." The woman. "Take the first left."

"We're on our way," Tony said, in a voice too low for the others to hear. "We're coming out hot. Be ready to roll."

They rounded a corner. All the bouncing up and down was making her dizzy. She wished she could lie down and sort through her jumbled thoughts. Her name was Liz. Price. She . . . algorithms. A chair that squeaked whenever she leaned back in it. Centre . . . Goodkind . . . Where was she? Who were these people? Revitalized?

They turned another corner. Her right hand bumped against the wall, startling her. Pins and needles made her aware of her legs. One jerked. "Stay still!" Tony said.

"She's coming back," the other man said, sounding distant.

"We'll celebrate when we're out of here."

A door banged open. The grip on her legs tightened. They were going down stairs. Liz felt as if she were on one of those bucking broncos her second cousin . . . at a wedding . . .

Another door banged open. "Shit." The woman. "Fidos are cutting off the east exit."

The bouncing stopped. "Fidos heading your way," Tony said, sounding out of breath. "Meet us . . . Cathy!"

"I'm looking."

Liz raised her head again. The woman—Cathy—still had her eyes glued to the gadget. "We'll try for the service entrance, but we have to hurry."

"The service entrance, but be careful," Tony told whoever was listening.

The corridor, which looked identical to the one on the

other floor, moved again. Feeling stronger, Liz kept her head up.

"She'd better be worth it." Cathy's voice rose. "Fidos on this floor. They'll come up behind us."

"Get in front, Cathy," Tony said. "Mike—"

"I'm ready."

Cathy brushed past Liz. Now she could see Mike holding what looked like a gun, but with a muzzle shaped like a horn. Beyond Mike, a security guard ran into the corridor. Two more appeared behind him.

Mike raised his weapon. The air seemed to crackle. Blue light arced from the weapon's muzzle and struck one of the guards. He froze in his tracks, convulsions racking him. Another guard thrust out his hand, gesturing for them to stop. Popping noises.

"They're shooting at us," Mike shouted.

But the guard wasn't holding anything. What were they shooting with? Was there something wrong with her eyes? She'd felt weird ever since she'd woken up.

Crackling again, and another arc of light. It hit the wall behind the two guards still in pursuit. "Hurry. We can't hold them—" A barrage of pops drowned Mike out. His left knee gave way. He hit the floor with a grunt, his weapon spinning away from him. "I'm hit," he shrieked.

Tony didn't break his stride. Mike looked in Liz's direction, his eyes pleading. "Don't let them take me," he yelled, reaching toward her. "Do it!"

"My hands are full," Tony said.

"Fuck!" Cathy. "Fuck, fuck, fuck." She was suddenly

there, her feet planted and a gun in her right hand. "I'm sorry." A pop. Mike's head jerked back. Blood trickled from the bullet hole in his forehead.

Liz sucked in her breath. "You shot him." Her voice sounded foreign to her. "You shot him." Nothing was making sense. Maybe she was dreaming.

Cathy spun and darted past her. "Left," she barked. As they rounded the corner, something zinged off the wall.

"That was close," Tony said.

"Take the next right. We should see the exit."

The corridor moved faster. They turned a corner and burst through a set of double doors. "Hurry," someone shouted. Cement. Asphalt. A receding office building. Then hands grasping, pulling her away from Tony. Liz landed on her back and stared up at metal.

"Where's Mike?"

"We lost him," Cathy said.

"Shit."

A door slid shut. "Go, go, go!"

Squealing. Liz's stomach lurched. A man stared down at her. "So that's her, eh?"

She passed out.

LIZ ROLLED ONTO her back and stretched her arms and legs. She wanted to savour another few minutes in bed before the alarm went off. What a crazy dream! A little more coherent than some she'd had, but crazy, all the same. Security guards shooting bullets from their hands. Some type of ray or laser gun. Being carried out of an office building. A woman—Cathy—killing someone who was apparently on her side. She chuckled to herself. Funny what the brain came up with.

A scratching noise caught her attention. Someone coughed. Liz's eyes snapped open; she bolted upright. A man sat hunched over a desk, writing on a notepad. "Who the hell are you?" she blurted, while a simultaneous shocked recognition stabbed through her. She knew this man—from her dream.

He twisted toward her. "Ah, you're awake."

She opened her mouth to respond, but the IV snaking toward the bed caught her eye. She looked at the needle in her arm, then at the bed, and the floral wallpaper, the dresser, a couple of rolling chairs, the desk, and the man shrewdly watching her, his pen resting on the notepad.

"Where am I?" she asked.

"Do you know who you are?"

What kind of question was that? "Do you want to tell me what's going on? Where am I? Am I in hospital?" Though she'd never seen a hospital room that looked like this.

He lifted his left hand. "I know this is confusing for you. Just humour me, please. What's your name?"

Maybe she'd been in a coma, and the man was a neurologist. This wasn't a hospital, but some type of long-term care facility. "Liz Price. Now it's your turn. Who the hell are you?"

He chuckled. "Personality intact, I see. What's the last thing you remember doing, Liz? Think back. What were you doing?"

She'd woken up and been carried from—no, that had

been a dream. Mom, holding her hand—no. Nic. Nic had fallen off her bike.

"I was cycling with my daughter." Maybe she'd fallen, and not Nic. If she'd banged her head . . . Her hands clenched. She wanted so much to remember how she'd ended up here, wherever this was, but she was in a fog. Every time she tried to recall the details, she felt as if she were grasping at air. "You haven't told me who you are. But your name is Tony, isn't it?" She'd dreamed about him, so she must know him, but couldn't remember in what context.

He nodded. "Tony Green. Dr. Tony Green, but just call me Tony. Are you sure the last thing you remember is cycling? You don't remember anything after that? What do you do for a living?"

"I'm an AI researcher," she said, surprising herself. Then it came rushing back. "I work at the Martin Goodkind Research Centre. I—" *My supervisor just collapsed.* "I collapsed. I . . ." She slapped the bed. Why couldn't she remember? "What's wrong with me? Are you a neurologist? And what is this place? It's not a hospital. Where's my daughter? Is she with my mother?"

"No." Tony leaned forward and met her eyes. "What I'm about to tell you may sound implausible, so just listen and accept it for now. It will eventually come back to you. You died, Liz. You had terminal cancer. You'd arranged to have your body cryogenically frozen, with the hope that you'd be revived when medicine was advanced enough to thaw you and cure your condition. That time has arrived. You were thawed yesterday."

She snorted, but then . . . She remembered filling out

the forms and changing the beneficiary on her life insurance. *Frozen?* Mom's surprise. Disney World. Jumbled fragments. Nic. Nic and Mom must be . . . Her chest ached. She wouldn't think about them now. She needed to focus, to find out how long she'd been frozen and where she was.

"Your memory will be fully restored over time. You remember your work and your daughter. You're doing well."

She surveyed the room again. "This looks exactly like a room in the twenty-first century." Were the furnishings for her benefit? Was she in a facility that acclimatized those from the past with the present? "What year is it? How long—"

Someone knocked at the door, then opened it. "I thought I heard voices," the new arrival said.

Liz stared at the woman who stepped into the room. Cathy? It suddenly hit her. "It wasn't a dream."

"What?" Tony said. Cathy looked down at her.

"It wasn't a dream. The escape, or whatever it was." *Blood trickling from the bullet hole.* Her eyes flew to Cathy's face. "You killed him. You killed one of your own people."

Cathy's face tightened. "It was a mercy killing. He—"

Tony sliced his hand through the air, cutting her off. "One thing at a time. I've only just told her about being frozen."

"Oh." Cathy slipped her hands into her jeans pockets. Jeans? Cathy and Tony wouldn't be out of place in Liz's time. The clothing was perfect. They'd done their homework.

"Do you remember androids?" Cathy asked.

"I should hope so," Liz said. "I worked with them."

"I bet you had high hopes for them."

"Cathy," Tony said, a warning edge to his voice.

"Okay, okay." Cathy's eyes were as hard as flint. "It's just that, yeah, we lost Mike getting her out, when she's the reason we're in this mess."

"She couldn't have known."

"No? I thought she was supposed to be brilliant."

"Do you mind not talking about me as if I'm not here?" Liz said. "What mess? What the hell am I supposed to have done?"

Tony frowned. "You need to regain more of your memory. Then we'll tell you everything."

"We? Who's we?" She sighed when he shook his head, but hopefully she wouldn't have to wait too long for answers. The fog was already lifting. Her office, her townhouse, the Starbucks on the corner, her car . . .

She remembered riding her bike with Nic, the fall, Nic's wounded knee. Snatches of places, conversations, and events, but her childhood, high school . . . she knew she'd gone to high school, but couldn't recall any details. What about university? She must have a degree, given her work.

Only Liz's memory was sluggish. Her mind was as sharp as ever. She understood everything Tony and Cathy had said and could name all the furniture in the room. Her research was coming back to her. *I bet you had high hopes for them.* Yes, she had.

Anxiety snaked through her. There had been plenty of detractors spouting doomsday scenarios. A machine super army obviously hadn't annihilated the human race, but these people believed something had gone wrong.

Everyone turned toward the doorway when the floor creaked beyond it. A tall, slender woman came into the room. Liz instantly felt drawn to her. As she had with Tony, she had a feeling she knew the woman, but this time she was certain she'd never seen her before.

The woman appeared to be in her thirties and had bright, intelligent eyes. She nodded to Tony and Cathy, her gaze never leaving Liz's face. The fascination was mutual.

Tony rolled back his chair and grabbed the notepad from the desk. "We'll be downstairs," he said, gesturing for Cathy to follow him. The door closed behind them. Liz and the newcomer stared at each other.

"I know you," Liz said, feeling both eager and fearful.

"Yes, you do." The woman rolled a chair closer to the bed and sat down. She clasped her hands on her lap. "My name is Nicola Price. I'm your daughter."

CHAPTER THREE

L IZ STUDIED THE woman seated at her bedside. "My daughter," was all she could whisper, trying to comprehend, to accept, the woman's shocking words. "How old are you?"

"Thirty-four."

Her mind went where it always did when she was off balance and unsure: to the rational. She did the math. "Then I wasn't frozen for long."

"Twenty-seven years."

A multitude of questions crowded Liz's mind. "Where's Nana? Your grandmother."

The woman—Nic—looked down at her lap. "Nan. I called her Nan when I was older."

Liz's stomach knotted. "Called?"

"She passed away three years ago."

What? Mom had been as fit as an ox. She'd had a good thirty years ahead of her, at least. "What happened?"

Nic lifted her head. "I'll tell you when the answer will make sense."

"I'm not addled. I'm missing pieces of my life, but I'm all here."

"You've missed over twenty-five years. Things have changed."

"What things? Tell me."

"I want you to rest for a few days. Then we'll talk."

"You're not my doctor."

"Tony wants you to rest, too. You weren't revitalized under the best of conditions. You're doing well, but we don't want to take any chances."

Liz had made an assumption—a faulty one, it turned out. She'd assumed Nic had been called here because she was a living relative. She hadn't considered the possibility that Nic hadn't rushed here because she'd found out her mother was alive again. "Do you run this place?"

"This is a private home, somewhere you'll be safe."

Safe. "There's something wrong with androids. What's happened? Are they sentient?"

Nic hesitated. "Yes, but that's all I'm telling you for now, Dr. Price."

Liz drew back. "Dr. Price? I'm your mother."

Nic's nostrils flared. "I hope you don't expect me to call you mom. I'm not much younger than you are."

But Nic was still her daughter. "Fine. Call me Liz, then. Do you still go by Nic, or is it Nicola, now that you're all grown up?"

"Nic," Nic said grudgingly.

Why was Nic being so cold? Was it because of the machines, or androids, or whatever they called them today? Liz wanted to fold her arms, but she didn't want to knock the IV out. Cathy blamed her for something. Perhaps Nic did, too. "Do you remember our last bike ride, when you fell off your bike and scraped your knee?" she asked, hoping the question would evoke some sign that her daughter felt something toward her.

Nic's brow furrowed, and her mouth pressed into a thin line. Liz inwardly sighed. She wanted to take Nic's hand and ask her about her life, what she did, was she married, did she have children. But Nic's hands were clasped on her lap, her knuckles white. Liz didn't want to find out if Nic would unclasp her hands to grab her mother's hand, or slap it away. She couldn't resist a question, though. "What can you tell me about yourself that won't freak me out?"

Nic shot up from the chair and shoved it back so violently, it almost fell over. "I'll be back in a couple of days. Please do what Tony tells you to do. We lost a good person, bringing you here."

"You're not leaving already? Can't you stay for a bit?"

"I have things to do." Nic whirled when she reached the door. "We never went on a bike ride. We never did much of anything together." She yanked the door open and marched from the room, leaving Liz with more questions than answers.

NIC STRODE INTO the living room, then wished she'd quietly slipped away. Tony and Cathy gazed at her, sympathy and curiosity in their eyes. "Are you okay?" Tony asked.

"Fine," she snapped. *Deep breath.* She forced a smile. "It's a bit strange, but it's new." Still, she hadn't expected it to rattle her this much. She'd had a couple of years to prepare herself, from the moment Cyn had broached the subject of enlisting her dead mother's help, until today. Months of planning: finding out where Dr. Price was stored, how to get to her without alerting any fidos, how to thaw, revitalize, and stabilize her as quickly as possible, and how to get her here, where she'd hopefully remember who she was, and more importantly, her work.

Nic had believed she could handle seeing the mother she'd known for seven short years, the woman her nana had assured her had always loved her and would be proud of her. Others had remembered Dr. Price as a focused researcher whose career had been tragically cut short when she was on the verge of a breakthrough. She'd been so determined to see the fruits of her research that she'd tried to cheat death.

She *had* cheated it—for now. Nic had resolved to view her as an equal, to breeze into the bedroom upstairs, introduce herself, assess the person she hoped would be *her* breakthrough, and stick to business. But when she'd laid eyes on her, the frail woman with the face Nic could only remember with the help of old photos, she'd been seven years old again, and shaken to her core.

She had to pull it together. They'd brought Dr. Price here for a reason, not so Nic could put all her questions to rest. "Fidos came to see me. They may eventually come here."

"We're ready." Cathy cleared her throat. "About Mike . . ."

"He wanted you to do it." Nic swallowed. "If they come here and find Dr. Price . . . do the same thing for her."

Cathy nodded.

"What did you tell her?" Tony asked.

"Not much. I'll be back in a few days. We'll tell her everything then."

His brows shot up. "It'll be a lot to take in."

"I hope she'll help us," Cathy said.

She'd damn-well better. "Call me if she's being difficult. I'd better go. Cyn's waiting outside in the car." So Nic would have an excuse not to stay. "See you in a few days." She'd also see Dr. Price, a reunion she dreaded but wouldn't miss for anything.

CHAPTER FOUR

L IZ CONGRATULATED HERSELF when she made it to the other end of the upstairs hallway and back, albeit using two walking sticks for balance. Her strength was returning. If only Nic would, as well. Four days had passed since Liz had seen her. Tony was a constant presence, and Cathy popped in now and again to see how she was doing, but it was Nic she wanted to talk to, study, and touch.

She'd thought about her escape, or kidnapping, from what must have been the cryogenics facility, replayed it many times in her mind and concluded that the security guards were androids, and the weapon with a horn-shaped muzzle incapacitated them in some way. But why had Nic and her group snatched her away? Why hadn't today's cryogenic people revived her? Had the company gone bankrupt? Was everyone frozen in limbo? What did Cathy blame her for? What was Tony injecting her with every morning and night? Where was Nic? Why hadn't she come back?

She hobbled back into her bedroom, rested the walking sticks against the wall, and sank into the chair Tony usually sat in. An open book lay on her bed, a mystery published in 2020. She'd never had time to read for pleasure, and twiddling her thumbs had always driven her crazy. Her knowledge may be outdated now, but she had a lot to give and wanted to get out there and start living again, and hopefully get to know her daughter. If Nic hadn't already arranged to be frozen, Liz would persuade her to do it. Then again, what was the life expectancy now? They could cure cancer. What other diseases and ravages of aging had they overcome?

Tony was thumping up the stairs. She recognized his heavy footsteps. "I heard you wandering about," he said, "and I see you're still up. Good."

"Soon I won't need any medication. What is it you're giving me, anyway?"

He smiled too broadly. "Just something to help you feel better."

An answer that would make a politician proud. "What, exactly?"

"Ask Nic."

"I would, if she were here."

"She's coming today. She should be here soon."

Liz's spirits rose. "Why won't you tell me about androids? Are you afraid they'll come here—because the security guards who chased us out of the building were androids, right?" When he didn't answer, she went on. "I won't be overwhelmed, you know. I was always thinking ahead, looking into the future."

"I'm sorry, but I can't tell you anything until Nic gets here."

He was always apologetic but firm. Liz stared down at her lap. She jerked her head up when a door thumped shut and voices filtered upstairs from the floor below. Nic.

Softer footsteps this time. Nic strode into the bedroom, with Cathy on her heels.

Tony greeted them, then said, "Should we leave you two alone?"

"No, I think we're going for a drive," Nic said.

His brow furrowed. "Are you sure?"

"She needs to see." Nic looked at Liz with impassive eyes. "How are you feeling today?"

"Fine. I'm getting stronger every day. I was just saying to Tony that he'll be able to stop giving me whatever he's giving me soon. What is it, anyway? He won't tell me, but he said you would."

Nic and the others exchanged glances.

Liz frowned at them. "What is it? What aren't you telling me?"

Nic moistened her lips. "He won't be able to stop giving you the medication," she said slowly. "Without it, you'll die."

Liz felt as if she'd been struck. "What? I thought—you revived me. Are you saying you can't cure the cancer? Why would you revive me if you can't cure the cancer? That was the whole point of being frozen, for god's sake. So I could be cured in the future." Her breath was coming in quick gasps. She grasped the arms of the chair and consciously slowed her breathing. "Why, Nic? What the hell's going on?"

Nic was silent for a moment. "We've conquered cancer. For your type of cancer, we can turn the immune system against the cancer cells. But every treatment is unique to the cancer and the individual. We need to train *your* immune system to fight the type of cancer *you* have."

"Then you can cure me. Why won't you?"

"Because they control the medical system. They'd have to approve your treatment. The problem is, they don't approve treatment for terminal illnesses."

"They . . . you mean androids. Sentient machines."

"Yes."

The bits and pieces Liz had picked up and witnessed coalesced. "You obviously brought me back without their permission or knowledge. I gather you oppose them."

"Many do," Cathy said. "Though not overtly," she mumbled.

"Why? What's so bad about them? I don't mean to sound ungrateful, though I can't say I'm bursting with gratitude, given that you've brought me back without being able to cure me. Why did you do that? Why did you have to revitalize me now, when you knew I wouldn't be able to get treatment?" She twisted to look at Tony. "Except whatever you're giving me. The stopgap measure."

"Let's talk in the car," Nic said.

"Do you want us to go with you?" Cathy asked.

Nic shook her head. "Cyn's driving. Can you get up on your own?" she asked Liz.

Liz nodded. Even if she couldn't, she'd be damned if she'd let Nic know. She pushed herself to her feet and grabbed her walking sticks.

"Come on." Nic hesitated at the top of the stairs. "Do you need—"

"I'll be fine," Liz said. Slow, but fine. She didn't object when Nic stayed next to her, descending the stairs at her pace.

Outside, a light breeze ruffled her hair, and the afternoon sun warmed her cheeks. She blinked at the strange but familiar street. Nothing had changed. The cars looked a little sleeker, but they were cars. The houses were the same. She was in a typical suburb. After all, she'd died only twenty-seven years ago.

She followed Nic down the front path. Tony took her walking sticks from her, and she slid into the backseat of a blue sedan waiting at the curb. Nic sat next to her.

The woman at the wheel looked in the rearview mirror. "So you're Dr. Price. Welcome to the future. I'm Cyn. I'll be your tour guide for today."

"Just call me Liz," Liz said to Cyn's reflection.

Tony peered into the backseat. "Will you be getting out?" He raised the walking sticks.

"Put them in the trunk," Nic said.

He did so, and waved when the car pulled away from the curb. Liz stared out the window, questions racing through her mind.

"We brought you back because we need your help," Nic said, breaking into her thoughts.

Liz turned to her—and almost gasped. Nic's gaze . . . the dimple smack-dab in the middle of her forehead, the set of her mouth, her chin . . . Liz was instantly transported into the past, when her daughter had gazed at her with the same intensity, the same-coloured eyes, the same dimple, the same mouth and chin. And now that she didn't feel blindsided by the news that her daughter was alive, she remembered the tiny scar next to Nic's right eye and searched for it. A lump rose in her throat. It was Nic. The woman wasn't lying about her identity.

"We need your help," Nic repeated, sounding stern.

Liz shook herself, forced her mind back to the here and now. "You brought me back knowing it would kill me."

"It may not. If we had control of the medical system, we could cure you. With your help, we're hoping we'll—"

"My life is the carrot you're dangling? Help you and I live? Don't help you and I die?"

"That's not how it is. It just so happens if we can shut them down, you can also be cured. We brought you back because of who you are, not because you have a disease we can use as leverage."

But how fortuitous that she also had a terminal illness. "You want to shut them down," Liz said. "Why?"

Nic studied her fingernails, then sighed. "You had high hopes for sentient machines," she said.

"I'm not sure what you mean by high hopes. I wasn't hoping, Nic. I envisioned a world in which sentient androids would contribute to society and improve life for everyone. I gather that hasn't happened."

"Sentience has, but I don't think things turned out the way you expected them to."

"Is there a war going on?" she asked, even though she doubted it. There were no signs of a conflict, and humans would have lost by now.

"There are worse things than war."

"Like what?"

Nic's eyes narrowed. "What did you expect sentient androids to be like? They'd have consciousness, but what would they be like? How would they behave? Did you see us giving them orders, using them as a type of working class? Did you see them going to school? Would they go for job interviews and join the country club?"

Liz twisted toward the window. They'd turned onto a busier road. People hurried along the sidewalk, their heads down. The faces she glimpsed were grim. She looked back at Nic. "We were focused on getting to sentience."

"You didn't think." Nic shook her head. "You expected the tin man without a heart, or the stereotypical friendly android who wished he could be human."

"Instead of blaming me for whatever's wrong, why don't you explain what's going on and what the hell I'm doing here?" Liz snapped. She remembered the driver and glanced at the rearview mirror. Cyn's eyes were on the road.

"They gained sentience seven years ago," Nic said flatly. "Around three years ago, we humans were suddenly both insignificant and valuable. Though we don't know why we're valuable to them. We just know we are, which is surprising, because when they first gained sentience, all they did was comment about how inefficient everything is. They love efficiency."

So far, Liz hadn't heard anything that horrified her. "What's wrong with efficiency?"

Nic's eyes bulged. "What's wrong with—" Her voice choked off. She said something under her breath. "How about we put this in terms you can appreciate? Forget everyone else, let's just focus on you. You want to be cured.

We can't cure you while they control the medical system. We brought you back because we want to shut them down. We need your help to do that. Once we've done it, the medical system will be back in our hands. You'll be cured. Yay." She folded her arms and glared at nobody in particular.

Liz bit back a retort. Talking to this kid had been more enjoyable when Nic was seven. "Do you mean you want to turn them off? Destroy them?"

"I mean remove their sentience. Turn them back into being clueless robots that do what they're programmed to do."

She took a moment to digest Nic's words. Her daughter wanted to undo everything she'd worked toward. Were things really that bad? There wasn't a war going on. The androids controlled the medical system, and it sounded like they expected everyone to be a productive member of society. If there was less waste and redundancy, surely that was a good thing. She was either missing something, or it sounded like a case of childish resentment because androids were smarter than they were. "I haven't heard anything that would warrant you bringing me back. Don't you have AI specialists here? Why do you need me?"

Now Nic's eyes went to the rearview mirror. "Give it to her straight," Cyn said. "Tell her about the shit hitting the fan. She'll get it."

"Will she?" Nic murmured. She turned back to Liz. "You must have expected sentient androids to outgrow the algorithms. Wasn't that the point?"

Liz had expected them to surprise her, to learn, make decisions she hadn't anticipated, adapt to new input the way humans did. Beyond that, she hadn't given much thought to what would lie beyond the goal post she and her contemporaries had strived for. Yes, there were those who'd sounded alarm bells and written opinion pieces about whether sentient androids would deserve rights. Yes, the ethicists were agitating over problems that hadn't yet existed. She hadn't concerned herself with such matters. She was—had been—a researcher, a pioneer. She'd been after the Holy Grail. She'd left the hand wringing to others. "We were striving for sentience back then. It was one step at a time."

"Do what you want to do and let later generations deal with the consequences," Nic said.

"Every generation behaves that way."

"Well, yours screwed all of us. Androids are sentient, and they have nothing but contempt for us. The only reason I'm alive is because I'm not old, I haven't committed a crime, and I'm not terminally ill. If I was any of those things, I'd be dragged from my home, or prison, or a hospital, and within a week my body would be returned to my family with a hole in its skull and a brain turned to mush."

Liz frowned. "What do you mean?"

"I thought I was quite clear. They're using us for something, but we don't know what, because nobody they take away lives to tell us anything."

"Don't you talk to them?" Liz bristled when Nic snorted. "If you want my help, stop treating me like an imbecile. I just got here, remember?"

"Sorry," Nic murmured. "No, we don't talk to them."

"That's not exactly true," Cyn drawled. "We do have contact with fidos."

"Fidos?"

"They're lower intelligence models. They were the first real breakthrough. They're dumb, but they're, uh, efficient. Each model can do one thing and one thing only, but it does it very well. There are security fidos, medical fidos, administrative fidos, construction fidos . . ." Cyn paused while she turned a corner. "We call them fidos because the security ones came first. They're like guard dogs. They took over from the police and other security agencies."

"But their responsibilities have been expanded to include identifying who's ready to be hauled away and killed," Nic added. "The responsibilities of all fidos, not just security ones. They're always on the lookout for humans to take, but they don't work too hard at it. They don't have to. They have their claws in the processes that can provide them with candidates."

"Who expanded their responsibilities? Who's in charge?" Liz asked.

"The masters."

"They were the second breakthrough that happened four years ago," Cyn said. "They're probably what you were going for."

Nic nodded. "In the beginning, they seemed fascinated by us. They observed, soaked up every bit of research they could get their tinny little hands on, were able to rapidly move the needle in a lot of areas. They're the ones who cured cancer. They're the ones who first successfully revitalized someone who'd been cryogenically frozen."

Pride surged through Liz, and a smile tugged at her lips.

"As far as we know, there aren't many of them, but they control everything. We don't have any contact with them. We used to, but that stopped around the time they started taking people away and killing them. Any new laws, or anything else they want us to know, are announced to us by sending us letters."

It was Liz's turn to snort. "Letters?"

"There's no internet. Not for us, anyway. They pulled the plug on all that. You can get some stuff on the underground market, but if you're caught . . ." Nic pointed at her head. "Hole in skull."

"And we're only allowed to work certain jobs," Cyn said. "Mainly physical and menial ones. There are a few exceptions, but not many."

"Do you know what they could be doing with the people they haul away?" Nic asked Liz.

Not off the top of her head. She glanced out the car window to give herself time to think. They were on a busy road lined with office buildings. Downtown, perhaps. "Where are we going?"

"You'll see in a minute." Nic tapped her arm. "What do you think they're doing with the people they take?"

Liz turned back to her. "You said the ones returned have brains that have turned to mush. Have you done autopsies? Can you be more specific?"

"They were crude autopsies, because the requests the families made for autopsies were denied."

"Some humans work in medical facilities, but they're closely supervised," Cyn added. "There are paramedics, but every ambulance has a medical fido on board. You know, so if someone's not going to make it, they can keep them alive long enough for the masters to do whatever they do with them and then kill them."

Liz could hear the sarcasm in her voice. "Did the crude autopsies tell you anything?" she asked.

"Just that the structure of the brain had collapsed, and it looked as if something was inserted through the hole in the skull," Nic said.

"They might be establishing a neural connection with humans, but why?" Liz mused aloud.

"We don't care about why. We just want it stopped."

Liz cared. Removing their sentience would be a drastic measure. There had to be a way to find out what was going on and negotiate with the masters that didn't involve turning them back into mindless machines.

"That's not the only thing we don't understand," Nic said. "Around the same time they started taking us and bodies showed up, they stopped innovating. They stopped caring about anything. Like I said, they used to care—a lot. If we can get control of the medical system, we'll be able to cure you because they ran with all the cancer theories and research and ripped through probabilities and models faster than we ever could. We were optimistic. We started to believe that, yeah, this could be a partnership. But then, bam. No more research. No more communication with them. They put the current draconian laws into place and revoked our access to the network. Something happened, and it's related to whatever it is they're doing with the people they take."

Nic straightened and pointed out the window. "Pull over

here, Cyn." Liz peered out her window again. They were across the street from a hospital.

"Are you strong enough to get out and walk?" Nic asked.

"With the walking sticks."

"Are you sure about this?" Cyn said. "If they see her . . ."

"They made their half-assed effort to find her and now they're back to not caring. And she looks injured, not terminal. The disguise will work." Nic left the car and opened its trunk. She propped Liz's walking sticks near her door, then rounded the car and slid back inside. "Here." She handed Liz a pair of sunglasses and a wig. "Put these on."

Liz stared at her. "Are you serious?"

"If they're sweeping this area for you, they'll be trying to match you to a photo."

Depending on the sophistication of the image matching algorithm, a wig and a pair of sunglasses might not help. But to humour her, Liz slipped on the sunglasses and pulled the wig on. She adjusted it using a hand-mirror Cyn handed to her and tucked in all the stray hairs. "Where are we going?"

"Around the corner."

"I'd drive the car around, but there's no parking at that exit," Cyn explained.

Getting out of the car proved more challenging than getting into it. Liz didn't quibble when Nic offered to help her. It was better than tumbling out and landing flat on her face. A minute later, they'd crossed the road and made it around the corner. A van sat parked outside a service entrance, its back doors open. "Right on time," Nic murmured. "They're so predictable."

"What are we doing here?" Liz asked.

"We want to show you why we want you to neuter the masters."

"Neuter them? Is that what you're calling it?"

Nic elbowed her. "Watch."

Liz followed Nic's gaze. Two men rolled a stretcher with a man strapped to it down the ramp leading from the service entrance. They stopped outside the van— A loud wail cut through the air. Liz's heart hammered in her chest. A woman ran from the hospital, waving her arms about. "You can't take him!" she screamed, her cheeks wet with tears. "Give him back, you animals!"

One of the men motioned for the woman to move away. Two people on their way inside faltered, then resolutely carried on, their eyes on their feet.

"Give him back," the woman shouted again. Then she lunged. A billy club appeared in the other man's hand. He swung it. A *crack*, and the woman crumpled to the ground.

Nic stepped toward the hospital. Cyn caught her arm. "No! There's nothing you can do."

The two men picked up the woman and slung her still form into the van. Then they unstrapped the man from the stretcher and slid him inside. They rolled the empty stretcher back into the hospital.

"Those two men . . . they're fidos," Nic said, her voice barely above a whisper.

Startled, Liz stared at where they'd been. They'd appeared so lifelike, their movements smooth and natural. "I gather those two people will end up with holes in their skulls."

"You're a quick learner, Dr. Price. You're living up to your reputation."

The two men—androids—reappeared with another patient. Liz followed their every move, fascinated.

"I can't watch this," Nic said. "Let's go back to the car."

Liz reluctantly plodded along after her. She couldn't resist glancing over her shoulder a couple of times. She still couldn't tell, not from this distance, and would love to get a closer look.

"Do you know where they take people?" Liz asked Cyn. Nic's shoulders were stiff and she didn't seem in the mood to talk.

"No. I just know that whatever happens to them, it can't be pleasant." Cyn hugged herself.

"They take the terminally ill?"

Cyn nodded. "There's no palliative care anymore, no effort to cure diseases that can kill."

Liz swallowed. She was terminally ill. "They'd take me. Whatever they're doing, they'd do it to me."

"Yeah."

But she'd given them life. Not all by herself, but her research and work must have been crucial.

"Right now, they take the terminally ill, criminals, the mentally ill, seniors . . . anyone they see as weak or not contributing. We can't figure out why they won't take everyone. The only explanation we can come up with is there are so many of us that they can't, and the groups I've mentioned provide them with a decent supply of guinea pigs. But that could change. They could kill all of us."

No. If what Nic and Cyn were telling her was true, they'd want to preserve humans, not destroy them. They'd never take everyone, but they might slowly enslave them, dismantle society, give up the façade of allowing humans to have a "normal life." "It sounds like we vastly outnumber them. Are all the masters in one place? Has anyone mounted an assault and tried to capture them?"

They'd reached the car. Nic whirled to face her. "They're powerful. They dismantled the military, and it's illegal for anyone to own a weapon. We have no access to manufacturing. There's no research, no access to information about them, nothing. We're blind out here. We can't stop them from taking anyone."

Cyn's voice quavered. "They take anyone seventy and up, even if they're healthy and vibrant and still have a ton to give." She blinked rapidly. "Bastards," she muttered.

A terrible thought ran through Liz's mind. Was that what had happened to Mom? They'd taken her away and killed her? They'd drilled a hole in her skull?

"I guess at some point, it'll be anyone who reaches seventy," Cyn said. "Nobody will make it to seventy-one. They'll all be killed before then."

"Not if we can help it," Nic said firmly. She slid into the backseat.

Liz joined her and seized the few seconds they were alone to ask her a question, hoping her daughter would offer a glimpse into her life. "What do you do? For work?"

"I'd just finished my PhD in theology and started teaching when the masters lost it. I work in a garden now, growing vegetables."

A degree in theology? That wasn't what Liz would have expected for Nic, but then her daughter had been seven when she'd . . . died. She wanted a private conversation with her, so she could ask her about Mom and how life had been after she'd left them.

Cyn returned from putting the walking sticks into the trunk, and they were on the road again. "Now you see why we need your help," Nic said.

Liz could see that androids could use a correction. "Some of my colleagues must still be alive, and there must be other AI specialists. Why haven't you gone to them? Why do you need me?"

"They're all dead," Nic stated.

"They were the first ones to get the hole in skull treatment," Cyn added. "A few tried to go into hiding, but . . ."

"They wouldn't have been in the groups you mentioned," Liz said, her shock making her sound shrill.

"I guess the masters had to start somewhere."

"One of my students transferred to another program. Maybe he's still . . ." She trailed off when Nic shook her head.

"Did he publish?"

Liz nodded.

"Then he's gone."

Everyone she'd worked with flashed through her mind. Had they seen it coming? Had they tried to steer the androids away from whatever it was they were doing? "Why didn't they thaw me and everyone else who's still in a cryogenic state? We'd be easy pickings."

"I don't know," Nic said. "We're not sure they were aware of your existence."

"But they chased us."

"Because they detected the presence of Tony and the others." Nic fell silent for a moment. "They know about you now, though, and who you are, and your work. They've tried to find you. That's why you're staying with Tony and Cathy. A couple of fidos came to my apartment. It's the first place they looked."

Liz sucked in her breath.

"I wasn't in any danger. You weren't there, and I pretended to be shocked. I told them I'd had nothing to do with it, but I'd love to see you." Her mouth turned up at the corners. "It's easy to lie to them, once you know what they look for."

Liz suddenly felt tired. She closed her eyes and leaned her head back against the seat.

CHAPTER FIVE

Liz forked the last bite of cake into her mouth and surveyed those around the dining room table. Perhaps the car ride that afternoon had been some sort of test, or a rite of passage. She'd graduated from the upper floor to the entire house, and had hobbled around while Cathy and Nic prepared dinner, marvelling at how familiar everything was, even though she'd lost over twenty-five years. It was as if as she'd taken a long nap and woken up in some other family's house, except her daughter was here, all grown up. And Mom is gone. How? When? She'd try to grab a quiet moment with Nic.

She placed her fork on her plate and dabbed at her mouth with a napkin. Whatever Tony was giving her had beaten back the cancer. She felt great, and for a moment wondered if they were telling her the truth about not being able to cure her. Maybe she was already getting the cure, but they needed a bargaining chip to force her to help them. She agreed that something needed to be done, but suspected they'd disagree over the "what."

Nobody had spoken about the androids over dinner. Liz hadn't said much; she'd listened to the others talk about trivialities like sports and shopping, and had learned a couple of things about her daughter. Nic loved old movies and collected Bibles. But the sense of fun she'd had as a child, her easy laugh . . . gone. Replaced with worry lines on her forehead that someone her age shouldn't have. She still laughed, but not with abandon. Her eyes didn't crinkle at the corners, her cheeks didn't redden. It was a controlled laugh. Adult. Restrained. Punctual.

Cathy pushed back her chair and collected the plates. Liz started to slide hers back, but Tony motioned for her to sit back down. "Rest, Liz. Let the others do it."

But not him? A man who didn't help around the house, and tonight, Liz didn't care. The others had gone into the kitchen, leaving her and Tony alone at the table. "How much time do I have before I die again?" she asked him.

Tony scratched his cheek. "I'd say anywhere from three to six months."

She wanted to scream. It was happening all over again. "But I'm getting stronger. I feel okay."

"I'm giving you a virus that's been modified to kill your type of cancer cell, but it's generic and crude. The best we could do, under the circumstances. It's managing to stay ahead of the tumours, but its effectiveness will wane over time. We need your immune system to do the job."

She'd seethe about that later. Right now she was dismayed because she felt like a means to an end to Nic, someone Nic could use. She'd worked with her friends to thaw her mother, knowing Liz would serve whatever purpose she was here for and then die, this time with no hope of living again.

"I get that you want me to turn androids into mindless machines again. But I can't just snap my fingers. If they're not accessible and we can't access a network, how are you expecting me to do it?"

"Let's wait for the others," Tony said.

They couldn't come back fast enough. Finally, she'd get details.

The three women returned with coffee, tea, biscuits, sugar, and milk. Nic poured tea into a mug and added milk and two sugars. She set the tea in front of Liz and flashed her a quick smile. Liz's throat tightened. How stupid, getting emotional because her daughter remembered.

Everyone else made their hot drinks and settled into chairs. The tension in the room rose. Nic rested her elbows on the table and cleared her throat. "You know the situation now. You know why androids have to be stopped. We need your help to do it."

Liz blinked at her. "What makes you think I can?"

Nic's eyes widened slightly. "Your instructions . . . code . . . it's part of their functioning." She tapped her temple.

"Others must have done much more after me. We were on our way, but we hadn't made the leap."

"Your stuff is the foundation, the brain stem, if you will," Tony said. "We all know what happens when the brain stem doesn't work anymore." He was the only one who chuckled. "In a complex system, you can disrupt one part, even the dumbest part, and the whole thing breaks down."

"It's only a matter of time before they run out of what they see as weak or useless humans, and go after anyone, including children," Nic said. "We have to stop them before it gets to that point."

"You were shocked when I killed Mike," Cathy said. "They would have done to him whatever it is they're doing to the people they take. He didn't want that. You heard him. It was a mercy killing." Her shoulders hunched. Tony patted her back.

"If they need us for some reason, they can't do it to everyone," Liz said. "Junkies don't cut off their supply. The masters will need a substantial healthy population to keep the species going."

Nic's jaw dropped. "Well, let's not worry about it, then. Not until we're sick or old, anyway."

Liz wanted to smack her. "I didn't mean we shouldn't do anything. But remove their sentience? Don't you think that's a bit drastic? When one of us is acting out, we reason with them. We don't kill the person."

"That's kind of hard when they're not interested in talking to us, we have no way of talking to them, and if we do try to make contact, we'll end up dead with holes in our skulls."

"If you want me to neuter them," Liz said, using their term for it, "I'll have to contact them somehow. I don't have to talk to them, but I'll have to access their neural net. But again, neutering them is drastic. All they might need is a correction." Even that didn't sit well with her. If they were sentient, they had rights. They were a new life form, just not a biological one. Would it be right if someone came along and lobotomized all humans because they felt threatened by them?

Cyn was shaking her head. "If all you do is try to

change their behaviour, nothing will stop them from getting involved in something else that will hurt us, maybe even make us extinct."

"Whatever they're doing, they need us," Liz said, feeling like a broken record. "I agree there's the possibility that won't always be the case, but if we can somehow contact them, or at least find out what they're doing with the people they take, we may be able to reason with them. What has the government tried to do so far?"

"Government?" Tony exchanged a glance with Cathy. "They're the government. We keep our heads down and stay out of trouble."

"But you're not oppressed in the sense that you can't have lives, and good food." She gestured to the tea, coffee, and biscuits. When Nic rolled her eyes, Liz's jaw clenched. "I'm just pointing out that some people are probably perfectly content with their lives."

"Until they hit seventy or get a terminal illness," Cathy muttered.

"Like you have," Nic said.

"Everyone's been affected by them, directly or indirectly," Tony said. "They took my mother, and Cathy's parents."

Cathy nodded. "My brother will be next. He's turning fifty-four this year. Only sixteen years, and that's assuming he doesn't get something they don't want to cure."

"None in my family yet," Cyn said. "But my parents are in their sixties, and I know a lot of people who've been taken. I used to work in a retirement home. They're all gone, everyone I used to see every day. Now I'm a cleaner." She gulped down some tea.

Her throat tight, Liz gazed at Nic. She didn't want to know, but she forced the question out. "And who do you know? Nan?" she whispered. If Mom were alive, she'd be in her early eighties.

Nic sipped her tea and used both her hands to set the cup down. "They didn't take Nan, but they still killed her."

"What do you mean?"

"I'll tell you in private, okay?" Nic drew a shuddering breath. "I know people who've been taken—not relatives, but parents of friends, and friends of friends."

"Mike," Cathy said. The others murmured their agreement.

Nic met Liz's eyes. "Everyone knows someone, like Tony said. Everyone's affected. It's not just the killing. We don't have any freedom, not real freedom. One step outside the rules . . ." She shook her head. "If you won't do it for freedom and the weakest in society, do it for yourself. We need access to the medical network and a facility to cure you."

Liz would prefer that they tried to communicate with the android leadership, but she was outnumbered by people who'd made up their minds. She grasped the situation. They'd gained sentience. They were no longer dumb machines that followed instructions people like her had given them. They'd subjugated humans and were killing those they saw as weak or flawed.

She hadn't experienced what the others around the table viewed as oppression, but she imagined what her future would be like if she were cured and the masters remained in charge. No research. No lab. No exchange of ideas. Knowing when she'd likely die, but not knowing the how. That bleak vision, and the sadness in everyone's eyes as they thought about who they'd lost, was enough to make her sympathetic. Something had to change. But the all or nothing solution Nic and the others wanted, removing their sentience . . . there had to be another way.

She was here now, and she wasn't convinced that the masters couldn't be reasoned with. Excitement surged through her as she pondered the possibility of speaking to them, studying them, continuing her life's work. There must be another option between "do nothing" and "neuter them." She'd figure it out, as she always did. But she'd landed in the middle of an unsympathetic crowd. One step at a time.

"There's something I don't understand," she said. "Who are you? Are you part of a resistance group?"

"No," Nic said. "We *are* the resistance group."

Liz barked a laugh, then wished she hadn't when she saw the expressions on their faces. "You're serious. Why are you sticking your necks out?"

"Because I asked them to," Nic said.

"You're the instigator?"

"Yes."

Liz stared at her daughter. Nic stared back. "Apparently we don't have access to anything," Liz said, wishing she were alone with Nic so she could find out why her daughter was so hell-bent on undoing her work. "How do you propose I neuter them, so to speak?"

"When they shut down the internet, they didn't destroy computers and other gadgets, but most people handed them in for recycling because they were pretty useless."

"Except for hard-core gamers and other diehards." Tony

raised his brows. "Think back to the time before the internet. Not many people had home computers. Those who did are the types of people who hung on to theirs."

"And businesses, but what they can do is limited and monitored," Nic added.

"What about phones?" Liz asked "They must connect to something."

"Voice only. Forget apps."

"All right, if phones and computers can't be connected to a network—"

"We think we have a way to connect to the masters," Nic said.

"How?"

"If you agree to do it, someone else will work with you. He's not here, because I didn't want to risk him for nothing."

"What are you worried about?" Liz asked. "From what I've seen and what you've said, the androids don't pay much attention to you."

"Apart from enforcing the law," Cathy said. "What we're discussing here, that's breaking the law because we're talking about harming the masters. But in practice, as long as we're somewhere private, no worries."

"I'm being super cautious," Nic said.

Why? Was this man important to her, perhaps a boyfriend, or husband? Liz's hands clenched in her lap. There was so much she didn't know about Nic. "What will you do if I refuse to help you?"

Nic's expression didn't change. "Nothing," she said flatly. "But you'll die."

And she'd probably never see Nic again. It was a good thing she had no intention of turning them down. In the last twenty-five years, androids had made the leap. Liz had expected to wake up to a world with sentient machines, though not so soon, and not like this. Everyone around this table except her wanted to turn back time and undo her work. But if she managed to tap into the network, she'd be in control. She wouldn't have to turn androids back into mindless robots. She could root around, see if there were other potential solutions, even send them a message. One step at a time.

She surveyed those around the table, sensed everyone holding their breath. "All right, I'll do it," she said. "I'll neuter them."

Excitement chased the tension from the room. Smiling faces swam before her. Tony gave her a thumbs up, and Liz could swear Cathy's eyes were moist. But it was Nic's face that brought a smile to her own, the flushed cheeks, and the shining eyes that met hers without any wariness or hostility. Liz had to admit their gratitude and approval felt good, but right now, her primary goal was to be cured. She hadn't paid all that money to be frozen, only to be revived so she could die at thirty-fucking-eight again. There had to be a way to gain access to the treatment she needed and stop whatever the androids were doing without destroying what she and her colleagues had accomplished. She sipped her tea. It was still hot, but had cooled enough to drink.

"I'll bring Ben over tomorrow," Nic said. "The tech guy."

"Good. I want to get started. The sooner we get going, the

sooner we can find out what's going on and stop it." And the sooner she could make contact with the masters. She only had three to six months, and it sounded like she'd be going downhill for some of it. She wasn't expecting to connect to the network and instantly understand how to communicate with them and affect their behaviour.

As she drank the rest of her tea, the others discussed what life would be like once they were free of their oppressors. The conversation made Liz uncomfortable. She appreciated their confidence in her, but she didn't need the pressure. Then again, who was she kidding? They'd risked their lives to bring her back and had said she was their last hope. And hey, she was Dr. Elizabeth Price, a little behind the curve, but that had never deterred her before. If anyone could figure this out, she could. She would.

By the time she pushed her mug away, her eyes were drooping. She cursed the weak body that had taken her down pre-freezing and now threatened to cut her life short post-freezing. The moment she was cured, she'd figure out how to download her consciousness into an android. Maybe the masters would help her.

Nic would be back tomorrow. It wouldn't be days until she'd see her again. "I think I'll go to bed," she said. "I'm tired. I've walked quite a bit today."

Tony's brow furrowed. "I'll come up and give you your shot."

Liz slowly rose and said, "Good night." She clomped up the stairs with Tony at her elbow. After he'd given her the shot, she perched on the edge of the bed, gathering her strength to get undressed and throw on the nightshirt Cathy had provided.

Someone tapped at the door. "Come in," Liz called.

Nic stepped into the bedroom. "Is it okay if I talk to you for a minute, or are you too tired?"

"No, no, come in, talk." Bursting with curiosity, she waited for Nic to close the door and drop into the chair Tony usually used, then blurted, "Can I ask you a question?"

"Sure."

"Where are we? Did you move to where I was being stored?"

"No, that's a four-hour drive away. You were out for all of it." Nic moistened her lips. "You asked about Nan. She killed herself."

Liz gasped. "What? No. Mom would never have done that, unless . . . was she ill? Do you mean she had a doctor help her?"

"No." Nic looked away. She picked up one of the pens on the desk and rolled it in her right hand. "She was eighty-two. They'd just started taking seniors. She wanted to die on her own terms. I respect her for that."

Liz was at a loss for words. Mom had committed suicide? "How?" she asked, not sure she wanted to know.

"She jumped off her balcony."

"Oh my god," Liz breathed. Her eyes welled with tears. *Mom. I'm so sorry.*

"It's pretty common now. They have to do it in ways that don't involve guns, or certain types of drugs, because they can't get their hands on them. At one point, people could take sleeping pills and have someone tie a bag over their head or smother them while they slept, so no more sleeping pills allowed. People jump from buildings, like Nan did, or jump in front of subways or trains, hang themselves, gas themselves . . ."

Liz was about to snap at Nic, demand that she have a little compassion. She'd just found out her mother had killed herself, thrown herself off her penthouse's balcony and had time to think about it on the way down. But then Nic glanced at her, and Liz glimpsed the tears and pain that mirrored her own.

"I'm sorry," Nic murmured.

Liz wanted to go to her, lay her hand on Nic's shoulder or put her arms around her, but the gesture would feel unnatural. Was it because they were strangers to each other, or had it always been that way? She could remember a lot about her work; not so much about her home life.

Nic tossed the pen down and drew a deep breath. "People would rather die than be dragged away and violated. Cathy was right," she said haltingly. "She killed Mike because he wanted her to. We'd all want the same."

Liz's jaw clenched. Nic had better not be using Mom's death to try to manipulate her into neutering androids. But another look at Nic's face, and her anger died. "You were left on your own, then."

Nic didn't respond.

"Is that when you became an activist? Were you angry about your nan? Is that why you decided to do something about it, even though it's dangerous?"

"That was part of it."

"How did you know who to talk to?"

"A few of us had always talked about wanting to stop it. Cyn, Cathy, and then Ben—"

"Ben . . . the tech guy who's coming tomorrow."

"Yeah."

Liz hesitated. "Is he your boyfriend, or husband?" she asked, even though Nic wasn't wearing a ring.

Nic rolled her eyes. "God, no. I don't have either of the above. Ben's my brother. Half-brother."

Shock stabbed through Liz. "Your—you tracked down your father?" How? She'd left his name off the birth certificate and—Mom. Damn it.

"Yeah, I tracked him down."

Then Nic knew. Blood rushed to Liz's cheeks. She wanted to pace. She'd had one moment of weakness when she'd discovered she was pregnant and told Mom about an arrangement she'd kept secret for several years. Mom had promised. She'd promised!

"He was dead," Nic said, bringing Liz back to their conversation. "But I met my half-brother and sister. I didn't hit it off very well with Kary, but I've been close to Ben ever since."

So James was dead. Liz didn't feel anything except the usual twinge of sorrow one feels for an acquaintance who'd passed. They'd had a sexual relationship that suited them both. She'd needed him to scratch her occasional itch, and he'd wanted to play outside his marriage. It had been perfect—no strings, no sappy nonsense. Then she'd stupidly gotten pregnant.

James had always used a condom, and he'd done so

when she became pregnant, too. "Not one hundred percent effective," she'd been told, when she'd crawled into her doctor's office, told him about her positive pregnancy test, and demanded to know how the hell it could have happened. "Only ninety-eight percent, even when used properly." That was the end of her arrangement with James, and the beginning of a few weeks of going around in circles until she finally made her decision.

She looked at her daughter. "Nic, I had my reasons for—"

Nic's mouth set. "I didn't come here to discuss him. You asked about Nan, and now you know." She rose. "You look tired. You should get some sleep."

"I have questions, Nic—about you, and what you're trying to do."

"I'll be back," Nic said, already at the door.

"I'll see you tomorrow?" Liz said, cringing at how needy she sounded.

"Yeah, see you tomorrow," Nic mumbled. Then she was gone.

Liz had the sudden urge to go after her, to grab her walking sticks, almost kill herself in her rush to hobble down the stairs, and clomp down the path, begging Nic to stay and talk some more. But what would she say? She couldn't change the past. But she could change the future.

She wanted to be sharp when she met with Ben tomorrow. *Ben. Nic's half-brother.* She got into bed and turned out the bedside lamp, but sleep eluded her. She lay awake for too long, wondering how Nic felt about her and wishing she could have been there for Mom. Did Nic blame her for Mom's suicide, and whatever the masters were doing, and the way people lived now? Liz hadn't single-handedly laid the foundation for sentience. She'd been one of many, albeit one of the brightest. But she was the only one left, the only one who could steer their wayward children back onto the right path.

CHAPTER SIX

Nic hung her keys on the coat rack near the apartment's front door and went to the living room window. She didn't register the lights dotting the windows of the apartment building across the street. Familiar footsteps approached her, muffled by the carpet.

"You okay?" Cyn asked. "You weren't with her long."

Nic didn't turn around. "To be honest, I don't know how I am. Every time I see her, I feel pulled in five different directions. I love her, I don't like her, I'm curious about her, I don't want to know, I want to tell her about myself, I don't want to let her in." She rubbed her forehead.

"Not everyone gets to talk with their dead mother. Not in the flesh, anyway."

Any other time, Nic would have chuckled.

"Maybe we shouldn't have brought her back," Cyn said quietly.

"We had to bring her back. What else could we do?"

"You weren't crazy about the idea when I first suggested it."

Because she'd been afraid that seeing her mother would do exactly what it was doing: tying her in knots and making it difficult to focus on the task at hand. "The more you talked about it, the more it made sense. But it's not easy, and it's probably not easy for her, either. I don't know what's going through her mind." Though Dr. Price was exactly what Nic had expected: rational, blunt, and with a superior air about her. She'd agreed to help them because she wanted to be cured. She didn't give a shit about those being killed. Didn't she understand that she was a prime candidate for the experience? "She didn't have herself frozen because she wanted to find out what happened to me and my grandmother. She had herself frozen so she could see what had become of her precious androids."

"Maybe she had herself frozen because she didn't want to die."

No, that sounded more like the reason why a normal, well-rounded person would do it, not the single-minded Dr. Price. "When she died, I missed her. I don't know why. We hardly spent any time together."

"Because she was your mother and you loved her."

Nic swallowed. "I don't know. She didn't have time for me. I always felt as if I was being fit into her schedule, and I didn't get many appointments. And when she did give me the time of day, she was tense. Businesslike. We were having lunch once. I forget what we were talking about, but I remember how flat she sounded. It didn't matter what I said, she answered in the same lifeless tone." The memory brought back her bewilderment at the mother who'd given her everything except what she'd wanted most. "I wanted to take my fork and stick it in her hand, to see if she'd scream, or yell at me, or show any interest beyond making sure I was fed and clothed. I remember thinking once that if I was a robot, maybe she'd pay more attention to me. Then she died, and I thought, now I'll never know if she cared about me."

"And now she's back."

"Yeah. And I have all these things I've always wondered about, like why she had me. We got on to the topic of my father tonight. It would have been the perfect time, but I wimped out." She lifted her hands and dropped them helplessly. "I walked out on her. Why, when I've asked myself the question over and over? Why didn't I ask her?" She shook her head. "Don't answer that. I know the answer. I know it's because I'm afraid of what she'll say. God, I'm a wreck."

Cyn slipped her arms around Nic's waist and leaned her head against her back. Nic's tension drained away. She closed her eyes and covered Cyn's hands with her own.

"This situation would throw anybody," Cyn said, sounding muffled. "Give yourself a break. You two have to get to know each other, get comfortable. Then you'll talk."

"You think?" Nic didn't see Cyn's answering smile, but she felt it.

"Yeah, I think." Cyn paused. "Did you tell her about us?"

"No. I was going to, but then Ben came up, and I told her who he is, and . . ." She'd wanted to protect the most precious thing in her life. Would Dr. Price understand? Did she understand love? "I'll do it when the time is right. Everyone knows not to say anything."

Cyn lifted her head from Nic's back. "The time will never be right. You know that. Are you worried she'll freak out?

She died in 2018, not 1918. It might be a bit of a shock, but she'll be okay about it. You said her views were—are liberal."

Nic glanced over her shoulder. "If she gets upset about it, it won't be because you're a woman. It'll be because you're not an android."

They both laughed. Nic could feel her bleak mood lifting. See, this is what she wanted to protect. She didn't want Dr. Price poo-pooing her and Cyn's relationship. "At least she won't be able to take the high moral ground, not when she screwed around with a married man for years." She'd had two fucked-up parents. One she'd never known and never would. The other she'd desperately wanted to be close to, and now her mother was here. Could they be close? Was Dr. Price capable of warmth and love? "I do want to get to know her, as adults." Equals. "I want to try."

"I'm sure she feels the same way," Cyn said.

Nic wasn't so sure.

LIZ LEANED BACK in the dining room chair and folded her arms. The blinds were down, muting the bright sun. She gazed across the table at Ben, the tech guy, and Nic's half-brother. "I'm told we can't access the network."

Ben nodded. "They think we'll sabotage it."

"How do people do their jobs?"

"Most of us don't have jobs that require the network. Nic grows vegetables, even though she's a theologian. I'd been working as an electrical engineer for almost twenty years when the world changed and my job became obsolete. Now I work an assembly line."

Liz had a vague memory of James mentioning that his son was interested in fiddling with gadgets. They hadn't discussed their home lives much. They'd been lovers, not confidantes.

She studied the man sitting across from her. He had salt and pepper hair, and there was gray in his beard. He had James's nose and mouth, which meant he had Nic's mouth, too. James's youngest child was now older than Liz. He knew about Nic, so he must know his father had strayed, and with whom. James had always had a sense of the absurd. He'd appreciate that Nic and his son were working together to save the fucking world. What did Nic think? She'd arrived with Ben, announced that she'd make tea, and left them together, staring at each other.

"There isn't just one network, though," Ben continued. "The primary network is off limits. Only androids can connect to it. Those businesses that require a network have monitored access to an isolated secondary network. Getting access requires approvals, and more approvals, and only designated employees can use the connected machines. And believe me, none of them would dare step out of line because it would be traced right back to them."

Leading to the hole in skull treatment, Liz suspected. "How are you going to get me into the primary network, then?" she asked him. "You must have a plan."

He bent down to fish something out of the satchel at his feet and set a gadget on the table. "This is my plan. Well, that and the computer I'll bring over later."

She gazed at the black box. It was about the size of a

walkie-talkie, with an antenna but no speaker. A cable was attached to it—a USB cable, she realized. What computer would Ben bring over? A Commodore 64?

"Fidos communicate using a communications network that's connected to the primary network. The masters interface directly with the primary. I've reprogrammed this little baby so it can tap into the communications network."

"And from there you want me to get into the primary network, and from there, deal with the masters."

"Yep. If you can get in, will you be able to neuter them?"

"I can't answer that question until I see what we're up against."

"If you can, how will you do it?"

"Off the top of my head and with knowledge that's more than a quarter of a century old? Overwrite all the nodes in their neural network with something more primitive."

"Restore them to a factory default, so to speak."

"Something like that." She eyed the stack of technical documentation he'd slapped onto the table. "How did you get your hands on that?"

"My father," he said.

Her brows shot up. "How old is it?"

Ben frowned in thought. "He brought it home when he saw the writing on the wall. I don't know how up to date it was at the time. It was a little over three years ago. He died a few months later. Not too long before Nic's—your mother, uh, passed away."

"Was he taken by them?"

"No, it was right before they wiped out every AI specialist they could get their hands on. He had a heart attack.

Apparently he was dead before he hit the floor."

"I'm sorry," she murmured.

"Thank you. It's too bad Nic never got to meet him." His voice dropped. "I know he meant something to you. I, uh, I don't hold anything against you. Dad was a womanizer. I don't think he had a monogamous bone in his body. My mother knew about them . . . the women. I'm sure she knew about you. She chose to look the other way. Their marriage worked that way."

Liz stared at him, then snorted. "Are you telling me this to reassure me that you don't think I'm a slut or a home-wrecker? Or maybe you want to make sure I know I wasn't anything special to him."

His face flushed. "No, I—"

"Your father and I had an arrangement that suited us both. He didn't love me. I didn't love him. I didn't want him to leave your mother. I would have been horrified, if he had. There were no roses, no love letters, no promises made. When I found out I was pregnant, I ended the relationship. If it wasn't for Nic and running into him at a conference every once in a while, I would have forgotten about him the next day. Have we cleared the air now?" Not waiting for a reply, she lifted a bound technical specification from the stack of documents and flipped it open.

Ben cleared his throat. "I didn't—"

She lifted her hand. "I'm reading." Fortunately, he shut up. She quickly read the first few pages, and would have been surprised at how much she understood, if she hadn't written much of it. James had brought the documents home three years ago, which was twenty-four years after she'd been frozen. Twenty-four years was an eternity in their field. Breakthroughs and ideas had been coming hand over fist. Her work wouldn't have been replaced, but it would have been built upon, and should have evolved to a point where her fingerprints weren't all over it. Maybe this was an older spec.

She put it aside and reached for the next one, but dropped her hand when Nic bustled in and set two mugs of steaming tea on the table. Not three. Nic had already said she'd be off to work.

"How's it going?" Nic asked.

Ben glanced at Liz. "We've touched on this." He patted the gadget. "And I told her about how we can't access the primary network directly because they're afraid we'll sabotage it."

"Afraid is the wrong word," Nic said tersely.

Ben didn't seem to mind. "Okay, worried, then."

Nic shook her head. "No, what I'm looking for is, 'they calculated the probability that someone would attempt to sabotage the primary network if we had access to it, and concluded that the probability was too great.' They don't feel. They can't be afraid, or worried."

Liz looked up at her daughter. "How do you know they don't feel?"

"Because they don't."

"You'll have to do better than that. How do you know? We used to think animals didn't feel."

"Only idiots and those who wanted to abuse and exploit them believed animals didn't feel. When it comes to androids, we're not talking about biological creatures. They don't have nerves. They don't bleed. Anything they" —she made air-quotes— "*feel* is based on their programming."

"Can't we say the same for us?"

Nic's right hand went to her hip. "Seriously? You can't see the difference—"

"Whoa, ladies." Ben signalled a time-out. "As fascinating as this conversation is, maybe we should get back to working on how we're going to neuter them." He offered a sheepish smile. "We all agree they need to be neutered, right?"

Liz nodded, even though she hadn't decided what to do yet. They had to stop this taking people away and killing them business, yes. But remove their sentience—neuter them? She'd see.

Nic blew out a sigh. "I'm off to work now, anyway. My supervisor's sympathetic and giving me a long leash, but I have to show up sometime. I'll drop in later."

"See ya," Ben said.

Despite her exasperation, Liz managed a small smile and said, "Bye." Nic was determined to demonize androids. Liz could understand it to an extent. Nic had lived through a massive societal shift, and yes, humans weren't being allowed to live up to their potential, which disappointed Liz immensely. *Her* androids would work with humans, not dismiss them.

The front door thumped shut. Liz took the second document off the stack, then looked at Ben. "Why didn't you bring the computer with you?"

He swept his arm toward the stack of documentation. "I thought you'd want to read all this first. How long do you think you'll need?"

Judging by the last spec and the one she'd just opened, not long. "You could have brought the computer."

His eyes widened. "Really?"

"You should go get it." She gestured at the mug sitting in front of him. "Drink your tea, and then go."

He blinked at her. "I have to be at work in a couple of hours. I'll bring it over tonight."

She wanted to snap at him, but she needed him—for now. "When I was revived and carried out of wherever I was being kept, Cathy was using some type of gadget. She detected the presence of fidos. How did she do that if we can't access the primary network? Was she tapping into the communications network, and if so, why do we need your" —she looked down at it— "modified gadget?"

"She was using a proximity detector. The fidos emit a specific frequency. I rigged it up for her," he said proudly.

"You're quite talented," she said, deciding to throw him a bone.

He started to nod, then abruptly stopped and said, "Thank you," amusing Liz. "Anything else?" he asked.

"Not right now." She dipped her head and continued reading.

"I'll drink my tea, then."

"Yes, you do that," she murmured, not caring one way or the other.

CHAPTER SEVEN

Everyone gathered behind Liz and waited while Ben hooked up the computer. They'd all convened in her bedroom—Nic, Ben, Tony, Cathy, and Cyn. "We don't want the computer where anyone who comes into the house can see it," Nic had explained, when Liz had protested about having it here. She slept in here. She didn't want to spend all her time surrounded by the same four walls. But she understood.

"Ta da!" Ben straightened and swept his arm toward the computer.

It wasn't a Commodore 64, but it wasn't much more advanced than the one she'd had at work, either. There wasn't a neural connector she could plug into her brain, so she could think her commands. Virtual reality still hadn't made it into every home when it was banned. The monitor, keyboard, chassis, speakers . . . she was back in 2018.

"Are you ready?" Nic asked. "Can you do it?"

"What, now?" Liz turned to face her. "I've read all the specs. I can certainly find my way around the primary network, assuming it hasn't changed much in the past three years." And she was betting it hadn't. The masters had apparently contributed to many breakthroughs and innovations, and then nothing, except dead people showing up with holes in their skulls. If they'd improved anything, it would be security. She'd gotten the impression they were paranoid. "Do you have a plan for if we're detected?" Blank faces stared back at her. Great. "I'm good, but I'm not infallible."

"Can I get that in writing?" Nic said, to chuckles.

"You're right, we need an 'oh, shit' plan," Cyn said.

Liz smiled. "Work out an 'oh, shit' plan, and then I'll crack my knuckles and start digging around. I'll do my best to get around any security, but I'll be thinking on my feet. If it's radically changed . . ."

"If they detect you, will they know where we are?" Cathy asked.

"They'll at least know the general vicinity. I doubt it would take them long to pinpoint our location."

Cathy's brow creased with worry. She looked at Tony.

"If you'd rather we do it at ou—my place, we can," Nic said.

Liz noticed Nic's change of word choice. So, Nic didn't live alone. She'd said she didn't have a boyfriend or husband, but—could it be a child? Was Nic hiding a child from her? No, she'd said 'our,' which gave Liz the impression that she viewed whoever was living with her as an equal. A roommate?

". . . somewhere that's not connected to any of us," Cathy was saying.

Liz forced her mind back to the conversation at hand. "How long would we have to escape?"

"It would depend on where the nearest fidos are."

"We should do it where there are other people," Ben suggested. "A school, maybe? They won't haul away a bunch of kids."

"What about the teachers?" Cyn said.

"A library?"

"Same, except worse. They'd go after the librarians and the adult patrons. And we can't let anyone see the computer."

"How about the sewers or somewhere in the subway?" Tony said.

Ben picked up his gadget and waved it at Tony. "I need to be above ground."

"All right, it sounds like we need to do it somewhere with lots of people, above ground, and where nobody can see the computer," Liz said.

"Your van," Nic said to Ben. "We'll drive somewhere with a lot of people and do it inside the van. We can use a generator."

Everyone nodded. "What about the GPS?" Liz asked. "The van," she clarified, when Cathy and Ben threw her a quizzical look. "If they detect us, will they be able to track the van?"

Ben shook his head. "We've made sure the van can't be tracked."

"We had to before we came for you," Cyn said with a smile. "Otherwise they would have tracked it then."

Liz wanted to kick herself. She should have figured they were referring to the same van she'd passed out in.

"We could do it at the market." Ben turned to Liz." There's a market downtown that's usually crowded. We could get there early, park the van, wait until there are a lot of people."

"What about getting away?" Liz asked. "It doesn't sound like it would be easy."

Cathy studied her fingernails. "You sound like you're expecting to be detected."

"I'm being thorough, not pessimistic."

"We'd be in the parking lot. It's huge, with a lot of exits," Ben explained.

"Uh, what about the fidos?" Cyn said. "There's usually a couple of patrols in the market."

Nic's brow furrowed. "I can't think of any public place with crowds that isn't patrolled. Can anyone else?" Shaking heads and silence answered Nic's question. "Then let's do it at the market. The parking lot has a ton of exits, like Ben said."

"Who's going?" Cathy asked.

Nic pointed to herself. "Me, Liz, and Ben."

Cyn jerked her head toward Nic. "I should—"

"No. If anything goes wrong, you three will need to carry on."

"You don't have to go," Tony said. "They can do it on their own."

"I'll be at the wheel. I know Ben could do it," Nic said, forestalling any objections, "but we might want to move while they're still trying to tap in. I want to be prepared for that. He can't drive and help Liz at the same time."

Cathy shoved her hands into her back pockets. "I guess if things go south, the sooner you can get out of there, the better. Even a few seconds could make a difference."

"Okay, I think we've got a plan and an 'oh, shit' plan," Nic said with a small smile. "All we have to decide is when."

She gazed at Liz. So did everyone else.

"I want a couple of days to drill what I'm going to try into my head, and to come up with a few 'oh, shit' plans of my own." Though any plans she came up with could be worthless. If the specs she had were horribly out of date, she might get into the primary network, only to be immediately and utterly confused. But there was no point in telling them that. They'd brought her back to help them, not to deflate their balloon. "I also have to write the module I'll run if I gain access. And I want a bit of time to re-familiarize myself with this." She patted the computer. "I'll need to be quick. My typing fingers have to be nimble again. I haven't typed anything in over twenty-five years."

Their answering chuckles and grins warmed her more than she would have expected and evoked a twinge of guilt. They were expecting her to neuter the androids. While the module she'd write would have a chance of doing that, she wasn't sure if she'd run it. She'd have a second module up her sleeve, one that would provide her a back door into the network but leave their sentience intact. She wanted to see how bad things were before she decided which one she'd run.

"Today's Wednesday," Nic said. "Can you be ready by Saturday or Sunday? The market will be crowded on the weekend."

"Sunday," Liz said, wanting the extra day to prepare, but also cursing it. She was racing against time. Her body would shaft her again at some point. She looked over at the computer. "I want to get started. Now."

Everyone took the hint and started to file from the bedroom. "Do you need me?" Ben asked.

Liz examined the chassis, then hit the power button. Ben turned on the monitor. She barked a laugh when the familiar Microsoft logo appeared on the display. When the desktop had loaded, she was looking at a bunch of icons. "No, I don't need you," she murmured. She realized Nic had left the room and felt a pang of disappointment. But time was short. They'd have plenty of time to talk once this mess was cleared up and she was cured.

She sat down in front of the computer and flexed her fingers.

LIZ SAVED THE file she'd been working on, leaned back in the chair, and closed her bleary eyes. She was finished. She had two modules ready to go, plus a couple she hoped would keep the network's security at bay. But she was boxing in the dark. When the lights came on, she could discover she'd been fighting the wrong opponent. How out of date were the specs she had? That was the sixty-four-thousand-dollar question.

Someone knocked at the door. "Come in," Liz called.

It creaked open. "Hey, I thought I'd drop by and see how you're doing."

Ben. He'd visited every day since bringing over the computer. She opened her eyes. "I'm done. I'm ready."

His eyes lit up. "Really? That's fantastic."

She gave him a weary smile.

"Maybe you should get some rest," he said, his face suddenly filled with concern. "You look tired."

"It's not the cancer. I've been hard at it."

"Yeah, but you have cancer, and—"

"I'm fine." She drew a deep breath. "Can I ask you something?"

"Sure."

"Does Nic live alone?"

Ben's face froze. "Um . . ."

"I got the impression she lives with someone. She told me she doesn't have a boyfriend and I don't think she's married, so am I wrong?"

"I think you should talk to Nic," he drawled. "She wants to tell you herself."

Really? Nic wasn't exactly forthcoming with information, but Liz wasn't going to admit to Ben that her daughter was holding her at arm's length. "I just want to know if she lives alone or not. You don't have to give me details."

His eyes went to his feet. "I really think you should talk to Nic. Anyway, I have to go." He looked up. "You'll be ready for Sunday, then?"

"Yes."

"See you then." He beat a hasty exit, leaving her to stare at the spot where he'd stood a second ago. At least she knew how to get rid of him: ask for information about her own daughter.

She turned her attention back to the monitor. She'd check her work again tomorrow, after she'd had some sleep, but she was too wired to climb into bed and nap. When she'd poked around on the computer earlier, she'd noticed a Music folder. She navigated to it and scanned the titles, recognizing all of them. Ben had connected a set of speakers to the computer. Would Tony and Cathy mind if she played a track and cranked up the volume? There was one way to find out.

She double-clicked "Zadok the Priest" and stood in the middle of the room. She loved the opening of this piece, the build-up, the anticipation, all leading to the glorious moment when the voices swelled. Her eyes closed and her body taut, she waited for it . . . and then it happened, and she was caught up in the energy, the sheer brilliance. She was back in her townhouse, in the living room after a satisfying day at the centre, a glass of white wine on the coffee table. Nic would be upstairs in bed, using a pen light to read a story and believing her mother didn't know about it. *I knew, Nic. I knew. And all the people rejoiced.*

She wasn't one of those lucky people who got goosebumps when listening to a wonderful piece, but music was one of the few things in life that exhilarated her. It was orderly and logical, yet spiritual with a capital *S*.

When the track finished, she listened to the silence, still feeling the glow of the music, and realized her cheeks were wet. That had never happened in her living room, but hey, she hadn't heard the piece for years, and she'd listened to it after trying to find out information about her grown-up daughter. She'd missed most of Nic's life, and would miss the rest if she couldn't get through to the masters and figure out what had gone wrong.

The present situation wasn't what she and her colleagues had envisioned, but they weren't responsible for it. Everyone had known that once androids gained sentience, all bets were off. Some had worried about killing machines, but not this kind. It was up to her to save her work, and the work of those who'd come before and after her. If she couldn't, androids would continue to deny humans free agency and use them for some unknown purpose, and she'd die not knowing if the human race would survive.

CHAPTER EIGHT

THE VAN SWUNG into the parking lot and drove over a
bump, rattling the computer and generator. Sitting on
the hard metal floor next to the computer, Liz held on to the
back of Nic's seat and shot Ben a quick smile. Anticipation
and curiosity were keeping fear at bay. If everything went to
plan, she'd get a glimpse of the current state of the primary
network.

Nic killed the engine and glanced over her shoulder.
"You're on." Her voice was steady. "I've parked so we don't
have to reverse to get away."

Ben grunted. His makeshift connector gadget was in his
hand. Liz switched on the generator and computer. She'd
work here, on the floor of the van. The monitor and keyboard
were already in position. "You ready?" Ben asked.

She nodded. He plugged the connector into the USB
port and held it up. "It's connecting," she said, watching
the progress indicator on the display. *Success.* She quickly
opened the remote location and ran her anti-security module.
Nothing was kicking her out yet. She scanned the remote

node's root directories and files. They didn't match exactly what she'd expected, but most of the names were familiar. She tried to connect to the primary network and sucked in her breath when a connection was established.

Ben shifted. "What—"

"Shh!" she hissed. She was already having to tune out the roar of traffic from the nearby road and the occasional loud voice of a shopper heading from their car to the market. She didn't need Ben's voice intruding, too.

She pressed her lips together. There must be a way to hinder the masters, perhaps put them into some type of stasis, rather than give them lobotomies. She'd have a poke around before she made up her mind. She typed in the command to list the nodes on the primary network, hoping to spot the gateway to the masters. Only one node appeared. *That's not right.* She tried to get information about the node and received an *Invalid Operation* message. Had she been detected and the network was taking security measures, or . . . She asked for the network status and received the appropriate information. Okay, she wasn't locked out. She made the same request again, but this time piggy-backed a small module with it that asked for the current date and time, a low-risk, harmless operation. *Operation Denied.* Shit. "There's a problem."

"What?" Nic and Ben said in unison.

"They've beefed up security. The communications network has limited permissions to the primary network. I can't use it to run a module, at least not the one I have right now. It won't take it as-is."

Nic slapped the steering wheel. "Damn it!"

"It's not all bad. I'll download what's on this communications node, which differs a bit from the specs we have." The data could tell her how to give a communications node more permissions on the primary network. "We can try again. Just give me a minute." She initiated the copy.

The progress indicator crawled. Ten percent, twenty, thirty . . . It was at seventy-two percent when it stopped moving. Liz's gut told her something was wrong. She opened up another terminal to check the connection. *Terminated.* "We've been kicked out," she said.

Ben's eyes widened. "You mean they know we're here?"

"They at least know a suspicious connection was made to the communications network. Beyond that, I don't know what they know."

Nic fired up the engine. The van lurched forward.

"Turn off the connector," Liz said to Ben.

He switched it off and disconnected it from the computer. "I thought you had something to combat their security."

"I did, but it's based on the specs we have. I'm not surprised they got on to us so quickly. I figured that if anything had changed, it would be security. They sound paranoid."

"You didn't say anything," he said sharply.

She shrugged. "Would you have called it off, if I had? What was Plan B?" He answered the question with silence. "It wasn't a total loss," Liz said. "We got seventy-two percent of what's on the communications node. A hundred percent would have been nice, but we must have gotten something that'll help."

They turned a corner. Nic swore under her breath. "Fidos up ahead."

Ben peered over the empty passenger seat. "They're searching vehicles."

"Yeah." Nic took the next left. "Damn it!" She pulled over. "Fidos, again. They've set up a perimeter." She twisted to look at Ben. "I thought we couldn't be tracked."

"I doubt they're tracking us specifically," Liz said. "They must know which node we connected to, so they know the approximate area."

"You said they'd pinpoint our location."

"If we were still connected to the network, they could have."

Ben peered over the seat again. He glanced at the computer. "The fidos are searching for us. Well, not us specifically, but whoever connected to the communications network."

"Can't we wait them out?" Liz said.

"It won't be a static perimeter," Nic said. "More fidos will arrive. The perimeter's radius will slowly shrink. They'll search everyone and everything within it until it's completely collapsed. Buildings, cars, bags, pockets . . . everything." Her lips pressed into a thin line and she shook her head. "We're going to have to dump everything."

Ben's eyes bulged. "We can't! Do you know how long it took me to get the parts I needed to cobble the connector together? And where will we get another computer? One that works? It took us months to find the one we have."

"What else can we do? They'll eventually get to us. They find this stuff in the van, and we're toast. We'll be taken away."

Their shoulders slumped. Liz hated to twist the knife,

but . . . "Even if we dump everything, we'll still be searched. They'll find me."

"They won't," Nic said, the lack of energy in her voice making Liz wince. "Your fake ID will work."

"Won't they have the van's licence plate number?"

"I changed it this morning," Ben said.

Liz turned to him. "Where did you get a licence plate? Where do you get the parts you need?"

"I have to buy some of it off the underground market."

"Which is risky and expensive," Nic said.

Ben nodded. "But a lot of what we use is donated to us, to the cause."

"Tons of people are sympathetic to what we do, but too afraid to get involved," Nic said. "Giving us stuff and looking the other way is easy. If anyone noticed the van, they'll keep quiet about it."

"She's right," Ben said. "People let a lot of stuff go these days. They don't want to be responsible for sending someone to the masters. Nobody wants to be seen as a snitch, and the fidos don't offer a reward for information."

"What about threats?" Liz asked.

"They tried that," Nic said. "Last year they threatened to drag away people who didn't answer their questions. Some caved, but the threat almost incited a rebellion. We would have lost. Their firepower is just too great. But they backed off. If they didn't need us for something, we'd all be dead." She shook her head at the absurdity of it, then put the van in drive and pulled away. "We need to find somewhere that's not crawling with fidos."

"Watch out for CCTV," Ben said.

There were no windows in the back of the van. Liz shifted position so she could see out Nic's window. "What about behind that store?" she said, as they cruised past a mom and pop shop with a laneway beside it.

"It's too small. We don't want to implicate anyone," Nic said. "We need somewhere where lots of people go."

"Fidos off to the west," Ben said.

"They're closing in." Nic's voice lifted. "The mall. We'll dump everything there. It's not too far away."

The van picked up speed. Ben patted Nic's shoulder. "The mall's a no go. CCTV."

"Shit, you're right. What else is—"

"Maybe here," Ben said, pointing to an apartment building. "I'll check for CCTV first."

Nic pulled over. Ben jumped out the back of the van and sprinted up the driveway running parallel to the building. A minute later, he returned and doubled over next to the driver's window, panting.

"Is it okay?" Nic asked.

"Yeah," he managed to say between gasps. "There's a dumpster back there." He sucked down air, then hopped into the back of the van. They drove to the rear of the building and stopped near the dumpster. "I guess we have to do this, right?" Ben said.

"Yeah, we do." Nic got out and slammed the driver's door shut, making the van shudder. She swung open the van's back doors. "Disconnect everything," she snapped.

"Just a second," Liz said, deleting her modules and the partial copy of the communications node from the computer. She had a backup of the modules back at the house, but . . . "I assume a thumb drive would be suspicious." Ben had plugged one into the computer when he'd arrived that morning, explaining that he'd updated the driver his gadget would be using.

They both nodded. "Especially given what's on it," Ben said.

There went the partial copy she'd made. "We should scrub the disk and the thumb drive."

"We don't have time." Ben grabbed a hammer and magnet from a toolbox in the van. "I'll use these." He slid the computer to the doors, then hopped out. Wanting to help, Liz moved the lighter items closer to the doors. She carefully lowered herself to the ground, wanting to stretch her legs.

"I can't believe we're doing this, after everything," Ben muttered. He and Nic swung the dumpster's lid open. Nic tossed the monitor inside and didn't flinch at the loud crash it made. She stomped back to the van and grabbed the loose computer cables. Ben removed the hard drive from the computer. After smashing the two drives and moving the magnet along them, he hoisted the computer and everything else into the dumpster. "We have to get rid of the generator, too," he said.

Nic's jaw clenched. She dropped the cables into the dumpster, then helped Ben with the generator. They both groaned as they lifted it to the dumpster's top edge and tipped it inside. Liz jumped at the noise it made and looked around to see if anyone was coming to see what the commotion was about. Fortunately the building didn't have balconies.

Nobody came running. They probably didn't want to know.

"Get in front with me, Liz," Nic said tersely. "It will be suspicious if you're both in the back and nobody's up front." She plopped into the driver's seat and slammed the door again. "Hurry!" The moment Liz and Ben were in the van, she floored it. Liz was thrown against the passenger door.

"Slow down," Ben said from the back. "We run over a fido and we're screwed."

"Sorry," Nic said, easing off the gas. Liz gave her a sidelong glance. Nic's face was taut and her knuckles white around the steering wheel.

"When we get to the checkpoint, do exactly what they say," Nic said, her eyes on the road. "Don't say anything beyond what they ask. Don't ask them anything."

"We should get our stories straight," Ben said.

"We're going to swing by the market and buy something, so we can say that's where we were. I'd rather put us there than somewhere else, just in case one of them did happen to see the van. Got it?"

"Got it," Ben said. Liz murmured the same.

On the way, they passed within a block of several fido patrols. At the market, Nic and Liz remained in the van while Ben went shopping. Nic gazed out the driver-side window, her shoulders stiff. "I did the best I could, given what I knew about the communications and primary networks," Liz said.

Nic didn't move. "I know."

"We'll regroup. We'll come up with another plan."

"I don't know. I don't know what we can do now."

Liz opened her mouth to protest, then closed it. Nic may be ready to give up, but she wasn't. She had to figure out a way to make contact with the masters and get through to them before her cancer got the upper hand. She wouldn't deliberately get herself caught by the fidos, because that would endanger Nic and the others. There had to be another way to get to the masters, and she'd damn-well find it.

Ben returned with a bag of apples, some bananas, and a packet of homemade cookies. Liz would have asked for a cookie, if her mouth wasn't so dry. They drove to the nearest checkpoint, the tension in the van heightening with every block. Perhaps it hadn't been the brightest idea to forgo the wig and a regular pair of glasses this time around. When Nic had suggested she wear them for her fake ID photo, Liz had declined. If the masters were interested in finding her, they would have done so already. But now, with fidos searching every vehicle . . .

Nic stopped behind the last vehicle in the queue, a sedan with two kids in the back seat. Liz tried to see what was happening up ahead, but they were too far from the front.

"Remember, we've been to the market. Don't say anything else," Nic murmured.

Liz clenched and unclenched her hands. She'd memorized the details of her fake ID and supposed background, but what if the fidos wanted to verify her identity? If they tried to match her image to the name on her ID card . . .

"We're up next," Nic said. "Do what they say."

Liz tried not to show too much interest by sticking her head out the window, but when they pulled up next to the people—androids—fidos searching vehicles, she couldn't help but stare. They were so lifelike. She tore her eyes away from a fido's face and turned to Nic.

Nic had lowered the driver-side window. "How are you today, ma'am?" the woman standing outside it said, sounding like any woman would. Perfectly natural diction and voice.

"I'm fine, thank you," Nic said.

"Do you live in this area?"

"No, we've been to the market."

"I see. Do you mind if I take a look in your van?"

"No, not at all. One of my friends is back there."

"Would you please step out of the vehicle, ma'am?" a man said.

It took Liz a minute to realize he was speaking to her. She turned back to her window.

The fido's eyes were on her. "Step out of the vehicle please, ma'am."

She wanted to look at Nic. *Do what they say.* She smiled tightly and got out, then gazed at the android in front of her. She wanted to have a conversation, ask him questions to see how he'd respond, throw him a few paradoxes and see how he'd handle them.

"Spread your arms out please," he said.

Trying not to stare, Liz did so. The man patted her down. It felt like the many checks she'd experienced at airport security points, until he touched her bare arms. Shock almost made her jump. His hands were cold, like metal. "What's in your back pocket?" he asked.

"My ID and credit card."

"Show them to me."

Damn. She slid them from her back pocket. He barely glanced at the cards she held. "Thank you." Surprised, she quickly put them away, with heightened respect for Ben.

He'd pointed out that she should have some form of payment, in case fidos questioned them at the market. It would raise a red flag if she claimed to be shopping but had no way to pay for items.

"Do you live in this area?" he asked, mimicking the other fido.

"No, I was at the market with my—" She cut herself off in time. She was going to say, "My daughter." One look at Nic and he would have wondered why she was lying, even though she wasn't. She coughed and cleared her throat. "My friend."

"I see. Thank you. You can get back into your van now."

"Thank you." She gave him the polite smile one usually gave when saying thank you. He smiled in return, but the smile didn't reach his eyes. There was something unsettling about them, his eyes. They looked natural and moved realistically, but there was a fixed look about them. She had the sudden urge to stick her finger into one. Would the eye give, or would her fingernail break?

She got back into the van and glanced at Nic, who appeared relaxed behind the steering wheel. Liz could hear Ben answering questions behind her, then the rear door slammed shut. "You can go," the woman at Nic's side said.

"Thanks." Nic slowly drove through the checkpoint, then picked up speed. Liz let out her pent breath.

"We made it," Ben said.

"Yeah, but we failed," Nic said. "We failed."

CHAPTER NINE

Cathy, tony, and Cyn sprang to their feet when Liz entered the living room with Nic and Ben. She cringed at the hopeful expressions on their faces. "What happened?" Cyn asked.

"Did you do it?" Cathy said, a tremor in her voice.

Nic sighed and dropped into an empty spot on the sofa. "We couldn't do it. Not only that, we had to dump all the equipment. The computer, the generator, Ben's connector . . . they'd set up a perimeter."

"But that means—" Cathy whirled toward Liz. "What the hell happened?"

Liz stiffened. "They'd beefed up security. The specs we have are out of date in that area. I couldn't have known how to counter—"

"Months of planning, all the risks." Cathy threw her hands into the air. "We lost Mike. For what? Nothing."

"I'm sure we can—"

"If you'd thought about what you were doing instead of barging ahead without any consideration for what might happen, we wouldn't be in this mess in the first place. But no, you elitist academics never cared about how what you were doing would affect everyone else. It was all about getting your names in the fucking journals and—"

"Hey!" Nic jumped to her feet. "She didn't ask for this. We always knew it might not work. She did her best."

Cathy's attention shifted to Nic. "Her best wasn't good enough. Now we're further back than we were before. We have nothing." The two women glared at each other.

"Why don't we have something to drink," Tony suggested. "I'll put tea and coffee on." He brushed past Liz without looking at her. She followed him into the kitchen. "How much time do I have?" she asked.

He filled the kettle with water and snapped it on.

"I'm still improving. I can walk without the sticks." But she knew in her gut that how she felt, her strength, would be temporary.

"You'll be okay for a bit, but then the cancer cells will mutate and will overcome the virus. When it happens, you'll decline rapidly. On the positive side, you'll feel pretty good until the end."

Liz forced a chuckle. "Better than the first time around, then."

Tony's expression didn't change. "I hope we're not out of options."

She knew he didn't mean treatment options. "I don't know." She'd gone along with the plan they'd concocted. It hadn't been an unreasonable one, but now that it was out of the way and there were no more specs to read, she could turn her mind to reviewing what she knew. If there was a Plan B, she'd find it.

"Thank you," Tony said.

"For what?"

"For saying you don't know." He paused. "Don't mind Cathy. Killing Mike . . ." He shook his head. "We're all frustrated. She has to direct her frustration somewhere."

Liz wasn't interested in being Cathy's punching bag, but she liked Tony, so she kept her mouth shut. "Don't make any tea for me," she said. "This afternoon has tired me out. I think I'll take a nap. I'll be able to think better after I've rested a bit."

"You've been keeping long hours. Don't push it."

She returned to the living room to explain to the others that she needed a nap and to say good-bye. They murmured "bye" in return, except Cathy. If looks could kill, it wouldn't be the cancer that took Liz out.

She slowly climbed the stairs and had reached the second floor landing when she heard soft footsteps behind her.

"I thought I'd come up and see how you feel," Nic said.

Liz's mood lifted. Nic didn't hate her for what had happened today. She went into the bedroom, hoping Nic would follow her and stay for a bit. "Thanks for defending me," she said, when Nic stepped into the room and closed the door.

"You did what you could. Don't blame yourself."

She wasn't blaming herself. She'd worked her ass off, sucked up everything in the specs and written the modules in record time. But she appreciated Nic's sentiment. "I'm not giving up. There has to be a way to reach them."

"If there is, I'm sure you'll find it."

Liz wasn't sure Nic believed her own words. She perched on the edge of the bed. "Why is this all on you? You can't be the only one who's interested in shutting them down."

Nic shoved her hands into her back pockets and rocked on her heels. "Occasionally someone sticks their neck out and helps us. A couple of people came along when we broke you out of the storage facility. And some people hide people from the masters, like they did during World War II. We hid people for a while, but you have to keep moving them, and when will it end? We can't keep it up forever. I thought it would be better to deal with the root of the problem."

But they didn't know what the root of the problem was. Neutering the masters without having the full picture was a knee-jerk reaction, but Liz didn't want to upset Nic. She wanted her to stay, and she agreed with Nic's logic. Eliminating the root of the problem would be more efficient. "You still haven't said why you feel you're the one who has to do it."

"Because I have a connection to this whole thing in a way that few people do."

"What connection?"

Nic stopped rocking. "You."

They gazed at each other. Liz's determination to reach the masters increased a hundredfold, but she needed sleep before she took a run at the problem. Right now, she just wanted to talk to her daughter. "Maybe when we don't have to worry about the masters anymore, you'll let me visit you at home."

"Yeah, I hope to." Nic rocked again. "It would be too dangerous right now."

Was it that, or was she hiding someone? "Do you have kids?"

Nic gaped at her. "No."

"It's just that when we were talking the other day, you almost said 'our place.' I got the impression you don't live alone."

"I don't."

"I asked Ben about it, but he didn't want to violate your privacy. He said to ask you, so I am."

Nic moistened her lips. "I live with Cyn."

"Oh. I didn't realize she's your roommate."

"She isn't," Nic snapped.

"But you just said—"

"We're married."

Liz did a mental double-take. Marriage, man-woman, but Nic and Cyn were both women, so a same-sex marriage, so Nic was a lesbian, or bisexual. *Huh. Okay. All right. Deep breath. In. Out. Say something.* "Thanks for telling me," she said, keeping her tone neutral.

Nic's eyes narrowed. She pulled her hands from her back pockets and lifted them in disbelief. "Thanks for telling me. That's it? Thanks for telling me?"

"What were you expecting me to say?" Liz asked, confused.

"I don't know. Something that shows you care, I guess. You sound like I just told you it'll be sunny tomorrow."

"What do you want me to do? Be upset? I'm not. Surprised, yes, but only because I fell into the trap of making the default assumption about the gender of the person you'd marry. I should have considered all the possible permutations."

Nic groaned. "You sound like life is supposed to be

logical. It's not. It's messy and illogical and emotional. For most of us, anyway." She paused. "I'm glad you're not telling me I'm going to hell or it's not natural or something like that. But I guess I expected more than politeness. I guess I wanted you to show some interest in my life."

And Liz thought she'd done well by not freaking out. She wasn't disappointed in Nic, and she didn't think homosexuality was wrong or unnatural. At the same time, it had come as a bit of a shock. She hadn't wanted to show that she'd been blindsided. "It's not as if I'm not curious. How long have you and Cyn been together?"

"Six years. Well, we've been married for six years. We met in university, but we lost touch for a couple of years."

"How did you get back in touch?"

Nic's mouth turned up at the corners. "We had a little fender bender. I slid into her at a stop sign. I only nudged her. But we reconnected and . . ." Her smile grew wider. "Here we are, eight years later."

"You love her? You're happy with her?"

"Yes!"

"Then I'm glad for you. I'm glad you've found what you want in that area of your life."

Nic hesitated. "Did you?"

"What?"

"Find what you wanted in that area of your life?"

Liz searched Nic's face, not sure what she wanted to know. Was she asking about her father? Other boyfriends? Whether she'd hoped to get married? "What do you mean? You know I never married."

"Did you want to . . . eventually?"

"No."

"The old married to your work thing?"

"Not exactly. My work was important." She didn't like speaking of it in the past tense. She hadn't died again—yet. "But it was more about wanting to live life on my terms. Relationships are compromises. I don't like compromising."

Nic opened her mouth, then closed it.

"What?"

"Nothing." She glanced over her shoulder at the closed door. "I should let you get some sleep."

Frustration tightened Liz's jaw. What had she said this time? She'd answered Nic's questions honestly. If Nic didn't like the answers, tough. "When will you be back? We can't give up," she said, meaning it in more ways than one.

"We won't. I'll be back soon."

Liz wanted to say, "Nic, I'm dying. I want to spend time with you. I *am* interested. I may not jump up and down and bombard you with questions, but I'm interested." But she said, "I'll see you soon, then." Her shoulders drooped with resignation when the bedroom door clicked shut.

NIC TRAILED BEHIND Cyn as they walked to the car. Part of her wanted to cry. The other part was angry. Seeing Dr. Price always tied her in knots and left her wishing she'd handled the conversation differently. "I'll drive," she said, when Cyn started to round the car.

Cyn didn't say anything, but Nic could tell she was irritated. After they'd been on the road for a couple of minutes, Cyn said, "What happened this time?"

Nic kept her eyes on the road. "I told her about us."

"How'd she take it?"

"Like she takes everything else. Calmly. She said she's glad I've found what I want in that area of my life."

"That's good, isn't it?"

"Yeah."

Silence, then, "So why are you in a funk?"

"Because I asked her if she'd found what she wanted in that area of her life, and she said she'd never wanted to get married because relationships are compromises, and she wanted to live her life on her terms."

Cyn didn't say anything, and Nic understood why. What Dr. Price had said was perfectly reasonable, even commendable. She hadn't done what some people do: gotten married because society still made single people feel as if they were somehow lacking. And then they divorced, or made life hell for their partner, because they were ill-suited to be in a long-term relationship. Dr. Price had known what she didn't want and hadn't compromised. But . . . Her grip on the steering wheel tightened. "I wanted to say that parenthood requires compromises, too. I wanted to ask her why she kept me."

"You should ask her. I know it's scary, but you should."

"What's she going to say? She thought it was her duty? She was pro-life? What?"

"I don't know. You'll have to ask her, and you should. She's dying. You understand that, right? You need to ask her while you can."

"We can still cure her." Nic had no idea how they would, but she hadn't brought Dr. Price back only to have her die of the same disease. Dr. Price may not have wanted to see her daughter again, but she'd wanted to live, to see the future. "She's not giving up, and neither am I. We'll regroup. She'll come up with something. That's why we brought her back."

They stopped at a red light. Cyn turned to her. "You're treating her like an asset, part of your little resistance cell with a role to perform. She's your mother. If you want the mother-daughter thing, start being her daughter."

Blood pounded in Nic's ears. "I can't call her mom."

"Then don't, but you have her stashed at Tony and Cathy's."

"She can't live with us. They're not actively searching for her, as far as I know. But that doesn't mean they won't do a spot check every once in a while."

"Spend more time with her. Every time you see her, you last five minutes. You have to stop running away. Ask Rachel for time off. She knows what's going on, and she's always been supportive. She'll give it to you. We can live on what I make for a while. If we can't cure her . . ."

Nic's voice dropped. "I know." She might only need a few months off. Panic gripped her. She wanted more time with Dr. Price. She wanted her to live. "I'll talk to Rachel."

Cyn's face softened. She patted Nic's arm. "Good. Talk to your mom. Ask your questions. If you don't, you'll always regret it."

The light turned green, and they drove through the intersection. Cyn was right. Rachel would give her as much time as she needed. "I'm not brave enough to stick my neck out. I'm doing my bit through you," Rachel always said. Nic had told her about Dr. Price and their plans for her. *Their plans for her.* Not anymore. They'd come up with a plan together, and Nic would ask the questions that haunted her, scary questions with potentially scary answers. She'd wanted to show Dr. Price that she was all grown up, but the truth was, she was still a little girl wanting Mommy's attention and approval, and still afraid she'd never get it.

CHAPTER TEN

Liz looked up from the pad on her lap when the front door thumped shut. Cathy and Tony had finally returned to work that morning and had told her Nic had keys. Liz had spent the morning rereading the specs Ben had brought over and scribbling pseudocode on the pad. She'd figured out how to spoof a fido on the communications network, but she had a problem.

"I'm in the living room," she called out when Nic started up the stairs.

Nic backtracked and strode into the room. "Tony said you wanted to see me."

"I do."

"About what?"

Liz set the pad and pencil aside and started to pace. "You mentioned that fidos monitor areas that could lead to candidates for the masters. For example, they monitor hospital patients."

"Yep."

"How?"

Nic's face scrunched up. "How do they do it?"

"Yes. Is data sent to them? Do they physically monitor what's going on?"

"Oh." Nic's eyes brightened. "I don't know how they're feeding data back. But they do stuff like ride along with ambulances, hang out in emergency wards. They know how old everyone is. They're the police now, so they have access to criminals that way." She paused. "They used to have their hooks in the prison system, but now people convicted of violent crime are just given to the masters. They don't go to prison."

"What about appeals?"

"What appeals? They're a thing of the past. No more keeping a case alive for years. You get one shot, and if you lose, too bad." She interpreted Liz's expression correctly. "Yeah, I'm sure some innocent people have died with holes in their skulls. Oh, and mental health hospitals. They monitor those. They probably monitor other systems too. I don't know." Her brows drew together. "Why do you want to know?"

"We need to get into the primary network," Liz said, still pacing. "The communications network we hooked into is used by the fidos to communicate with each other. It only has limited access to the primary one. Some fidos must have access to other networks, in addition to communications. They have to receive instructions and send data back. The fidos in the ambulances might have access to the medical network. The fidos rounding up older people must have access to administrative records." She paused to take a breath. "Are you following?"

"Yes, but I don't see how it helps us."

"Get me a fido."

"What?"

"Get me a fido."

"You want a fido. You want us to bring you one."

Liz stopped pacing. "Yes."

Nic stared at her.

"Can you do it?"

"Uh, maybe. I haven't given it any thought."

"Start giving it thought."

Nic dropped onto the sofa. "They're armed. They usually travel in pairs, or in a patrol. They're like people in the sense that if they run into trouble, they'll try to get away or phone home."

"Usually travel in pairs. When don't they?"

"I think there's only one in an ambulance."

"Let's work with that, then."

"Whoa." Nic held up her hand. "Let's pretend for a moment that we can get our hands on a fido. Kidnap one, because that's what we'd be doing. It'll phone home."

"Not if we stop it." Liz sat on the sofa next to Nic. "We have a few problems to solve. How to get a fido, how to keep it without them noticing, how to use it to get to the primary network. We might need its cooperation."

Nic frowned. "Forget it."

"No, I won't forget it. They may not be bright, but they're sentient. They can make their own decisions."

"I wouldn't count on one helping you. They have no reason to go against their superiors. The masters destroy fidos they believe are malfunctioning or disobeying orders. And I've seen a couple self-destruct."

Liz's interest sharpened. "Self-destruct? Did they blow up, or shut down? Did other fidos come and collect whatever was left, or were they left for garbage?" When Nic looked overwhelmed, she said, "Sorry, I know you have to get to work." Her lunch hour was probably just that—an hour. "Can you come over again later? We have to talk more about this, put together a plan."

"Actually, I'm not going back to work. I'm taking some time off. We need to do this . . . neuter them. So until we do, I'm here to help."

Liz didn't have to force a smile. "Great. I'm glad."

"Really?"

"Of course." And not because they'd have a better chance of getting access to the medical system and curing her. Not entirely.

Nic grinned, then gave her a guarded look. "You could have asked Cathy or Tony about the fidos."

"I know." She'd let Nic read into that whatever she liked.

"I'll call Cyn, tell her to come here after work, pick up some dinner. I'll give Cathy a heads-up, too." She pulled out her phone. "Oh, and we'll need Ben."

A potential plan was already forming in Liz's mind. She'd discuss it with Nic, see if it was feasible. And she looked forward to dinner with everyone. Normally, once she'd decided on a course of action, she wouldn't want to sit and eat and make chit-chat for an hour. She'd sit upstairs, typing code with one hand and absently feeding herself with the other. But Cyn would be at dinner. Liz wanted to get to know the woman who'd married her daughter.

* * * * *

"LET ME GET this straight," Cathy said. "You want to lure a fido here by calling in a heart attack or something? Then, when it's here, we're going to hope the paramedics don't mind that we'll incapacitate it and haul it away?"

"Not here," Nic said. "We'll do it somewhere public, but not crowded."

Liz looked at the incredulous faces around the table. Fortunately Nic had waited until after dinner to tell everyone about the plan. It might have put them off their food.

Cyn shifted in her chair. "Start from the beginning and give us details. Won't they come looking for it?"

"Not if Liz can work her magic. She's going to . . ." Nic turned to her. "Why don't you tell it?"

Liz sipped her tea. "The fido will come in the ambulance. Nic will use an immobilizer to paralyze it." She'd asked Nic about the weapon that had a horn-shaped muzzle, and Nic had explained that it temporarily shut down several of a fido's systems, including its mobility. "Ben invented it," Nic had said. "He's bright, you know." Nic and Ben's father had been, too. Liz wouldn't have slept with an idiot, and she certainly wouldn't have had his child. She may not have been planning to run away with James, but she'd had her standards.

"Once it's immobilized, I'll put it into sleep mode, access its neural network, and make a few alterations. It will report that it's going to self-destruct, so when it disappears off the grid, they won't come looking for it. Nic told me they never do, that the trash people haul it away." Which had surprised Liz. She'd figured the masters would be afraid of humans learning about them through the debris and using the information to bring them down, until Nic had explained that the fidos blew into millions of tiny little pieces that cleaners swept up. "I'll use the fido to tap into the primary network. That's the plan. To make it work, we'll need a way to plug into a fido's neural network."

Ben barked a laugh. "That's like saying we want to rob a bank, and we can't take any firearms with us, but that's not a problem because the employees will give us the combination to the safe when we ask them nicely. There's a lot that can go wrong with that plan, if we can even get it off the ground. What will you need to plug in?"

"Ideally I'd have an up-to-date fido spec to answer that question."

"Sounds like that's the first step," Tony said quietly. "Any ideas?"

The others fell silent. "Your dad didn't have anything?" Cyn said, looking at Ben, not Nic, Liz noted with interest.

"I brought over everything he had."

"There's an older fido spec in the stuff Ben gave me," Liz said. "But the communications network has changed. Fidos may have, too."

"They don't need specs, do they?" Cathy said. "They'd store everything in the network."

Liz shook her head. "What you mean is they need specs, but they don't print them out."

"Either way, we can't get an up-to-date fido one."

"I said ideally and that the fidos *may* have changed. I doubted we'd be able to get our hands on a current spec, but thought maybe one of you knew something we didn't. Since that's not the case, I'll wing it. While their intelligence may have improved, Nic says their appearance hasn't changed.

That suggests the hardware—their bodies—are probably similar to the spec I have. We'll have to assume the interface it describes hasn't changed much."

Cathy's eyes widened. "That's a lot of ifs, assumes, maybes, probablies." She grimaced. "I'm not sure about this. You seemed confident when you went to the market, and look how that worked out."

Liz opened her mouth to reply, but Nic got there first. "A lot can go wrong," Nic said. "The paramedics might balk, Liz might not be able to get in before the fido regains control—"

"How long will she have?" Cyn said.

"I don't know. We've never stuck around to see how long one stays immobilized."

Cyn chuckled. "True."

"After it reports that it's going to self-destruct, I'll remove it from the network, but we're talking about an intelligent entity." Liz raised her brows. "It could figure out how to connect itself again, even though I'll try to prevent it from doing so. Not until we want it to, anyway. It will become my gateway into the primary network."

"We figure since it's in an ambulance, it has permission to send more complex data back to the network," Nic said.

"Data I can piggyback onto," Liz said. "Assuming I can see the communications network and what's connected to it, I'll spoof another fido."

"How?" Ben asked.

"According to the documentation you gave me, newly-manufactured fidos undergo a testing phase. During that time, they connect to the communications network using a temporary test identification that's assigned on the fly. The

IDs are reused, and from what I can tell, are valid as long as they fall within a certain range. I've figured out how to quickly assign one and then change it if it turns out to be a duplicate."

Ben frowned. "Won't some type of alert be generated if it's a duplicate?"

"I don't think so. First, we're talking nanoseconds when it comes to reassigning an ID. I doubt they'll detect that a fido with a duplicate test ID was on the network for a blink of an eye. And even if they do, it'll be a test ID. But they won't. I'm sure they won't."

Cathy rolled her eyes. "Well, if it works, great, but there are a lot of things that could go wrong."

Nic nodded. "We knew this wouldn't be easy. We knew bringing Liz back would only be the first step, that more risks would be required. But if anyone wants out, now is the time. We need and want all of you." She turned to Ben. "But we can't do it without you."

"Oh, I'm in," he said firmly. "This isn't what my father wanted, not these monsters. If we don't fix this, what the hell are we doing, getting older every year, working to keep everyone else going, and for what? So those who aren't brave enough to off themselves can be dragged away? If this doesn't work, I'll be tempted to find a way to blow up the whole fucking planet."

"That'll be Plan C," Cyn said, evoking a few half-hearted chuckles, including from Liz. Her daughter-in-law was usually the one who lightened the mood. She also tended to cut to the heart of a problem, and her eyes softened or danced when she looked at Nic. Six years of marriage, and from all appearances, they were still going strong.

Nic caught Ben's eye. "Thanks."

Cyn nudged Nic. "You know I'm in. It's a crazy plan, but it's a plan."

"I figured, but you're allowed to back out." Nic squeezed Cyn's hand. "Just because it's my and Liz's crazy plan doesn't mean you have to agree to it."

"Like I said, it's a plan. And hell, you and Ben and Liz are in, so I'll stick with the family." She gave Liz a sidelong glance. Her mouth turned up at the corners when Liz nodded to her.

That left Cathy and Tony, who were clearly conflicted about whether to participate. While they whispered between themselves, Liz and the others sipped their drinks and acted as if they weren't interested in what the two would decide.

Tony told the group their decision. "We'll do it. We owe it to Liz to give her the best shot."

Cathy nodded, but Liz suspected she would have been okay with bowing out and had perhaps argued for it. She wasn't offended. Cathy's reluctance wasn't about her. It was about killing Mike. She didn't want more blood on her hands. It didn't matter that she'd done what Mike had wanted. Guilt had a way of inviting itself in and outstaying its welcome.

Nic's eyes shone. "Okay, then. We have a chance."

"Before you get too excited, I don't know if I'll be able to put something together that'll plug into a fido," Ben said. "I'll need to look at the spec, and if the components I'll need aren't in my stash, we'll have to get creative."

"Get creative?" Liz said.

"Try to trade someone for them, or get them on the underground market. I have one guy who knows me and supports what we do. He sometimes gives me a break, but . . ."

"And we have to figure out where to call the ambulance and what to do when it shows up," Cyn said. "We want to be in and out quickly, and we need backup plans, in case the paramedics balk, Liz gets in but she can't rejig the fido the way she wants to, the fido regains mobility while she's still plugged in."

"That last one's an easy one." Nic smiled. "We'd just hightail it out of there."

"The others won't be so easy. We need Plan Bs for everything."

Tony pushed back his chair. "I'll put on another pot of tea."

CHAPTER ELEVEN

L IZ HANDED BEN the tablet-like programming device he'd cobbled together that hopefully wouldn't fall apart at the worst time. She waited while he carefully slipped it inside a knapsack. Today was the day.

"Cyn's a great driver." Ben zipped the knapsack shut. "If there's trouble, she'll get us out of there."

Liz folded her arms. "I'm going in with the attitude that I'll have a fido in this bedroom tonight."

Ben smirked. "If you were anyone else, I wouldn't be able to resist that opening."

She couldn't help but smile. "What's so special about me? We're technically in the same generation now. You're only a few years older than I am."

"But I see you as Nic's mother." He shrugged. "I can't help it."

Did Nic see her the same way? A rap at the open door forestalled any answer. Nic hovered in the doorway. "You ready?"

"Ready as we'll ever be," Ben said.

"Would you mind giving me and Liz a moment alone?" Nic said.

"Sure." Ben picked up the knapsack. "Take your time." He closed the door behind him.

Liz sat on the bed and searched Nic's face. "What is it?"

Nic grimaced. "We don't know what's going to happen. I think we can pull it off, but just in case something goes wrong . . ." She squared her shoulders. "I want to ask you a question. Well, I have lots of questions, like were you aware of anything when you were dead, but I'll save that one."

"A more burning question than whether there's life after death." Liz crossed her legs and leaned forward. "I'm intrigued."

Nic's apprehensive expression didn't change. "Why did you keep me?" she asked, her voice almost a whisper.

Liz blinked at her. "Why did I keep you?" she repeated slowly.

"When you found out you were pregnant. Why did you go through with it? You could have had a termination, or given me up for adoption."

"I wasn't giving you up for adoption. If I was going to carry you for nine months, I was damn-well going to keep you."

"But you didn't have to carry me."

"No, I didn't." Liz gazed at her daughter, wondering how honest she should be. The answer was important to Nic, which surprised her. She'd obviously wanted her, or she would have had an abortion. Though when she'd seen the positive test and the visit to the doctor had confirmed it, she hadn't been overjoyed. Far from it. "I wasn't expecting to get pregnant. I wouldn't have chosen it. But when it happened, I wanted you. I considered the alternatives, but I rejected them."

"Why?" Nic sounded curious, not judgemental. "Your work was so important to you. I was in the way."

"You were never in the way," Liz said firmly. "But you're right, my work was important to me. Being a researcher came naturally to me. Being a mother didn't. Doesn't," she quickly amended. "I could have done better. When I was diagnosed, I had regrets."

"We didn't spend much time together, even after you were diagnosed."

"I know." But she wouldn't apologize, explain, or defend. The past was the past. "If we manage to get rid of this stubborn cancer, I hope we'll spend lots of time together. I'm grateful for this second chance with you. I do love you." There, she'd said it, and felt as if she'd exposed her belly to someone holding a gigantic sword.

Nic's eyes moistened. "I love you, too."

Damn, she could feel her own eyes welling. She stood and brushed imaginary lint off her pants. "We should go. They're waiting for us."

When Liz reached the door, Nic said, "You didn't answer the why. Why did you decide to have me?"

Liz turned to her. "I told you, I wanted you."

"But why?"

Irritation flared. She waited for it to flicker out. This would be a terrible time to snap at Nic. "I don't know. I just knew I did. It felt right. I considered a termination, and there would have been nothing wrong with doing it, but every time I thought about making an appointment, I didn't want to. I didn't analyze why." For once in her life, she'd rolled with it and had never rued her decision. Her regrets had to do with her shortcomings as a mother. She'd never regretted Nic. Ever. "I made the right decision. I may not be a great mother, but I am your mother, and I wanted to be your mother."

If their plan was going to work, she needed to regain her equilibrium, clear her mind and still her emotions. She pulled open the door and left the room without looking over her shoulder.

NIC WAS GLAD she was riding up front with Cyn, rather than in the back of the van with Dr. Price, Ben, and Cathy. She had an answer to the question that had dogged her all her life, an answer that had left her wondering. Did Dr. Price really not know? Had she lied to protect her daughter's feelings, or was there a trace of maternal instinct within her after all, enough to make her want to raise a child, but not enough to pay much attention to her?

"Almost there," Cyn murmured.

Nic straightened and tried to mentally review the plan, but the conversation with Dr. Price kept intruding. In hindsight, asking her right before they'd try to kidnap a fido hadn't been a great idea, but Nic had lain awake last night worrying about what they were about to do. If she hadn't asked her, right now she'd be wishing she had. She couldn't be indifferent to Dr. Price, couldn't pretend she didn't care. *I am your mother, and I wanted to be your mother.* And Dr. Price had said, "I do love you."

Renewed determination surged through her. She wanted more time with Dr. Price . . . with Liz. They were going to capture this fido. If they failed, they'd try again, come up with a Plan C, and D, and E, until they got Liz the treatment she needed. Come hell or high water, they would have more time together, in a world that wasn't ruled by machines.

Cyn drove into the parking lot behind a furniture store and stopped the van where she had a clear route back to the street. Nic hopped out and opened the back doors. "Let's do it."

Cathy climbed out. "Are you sure they'll fall for it?"

"They won't know until they get here that you're not actually having a heart attack."

"When will you hit the fido?"

"As soon as it's out of the ambulance. If I tell you to get back into the van, do it. We might get the one tight-assed paramedic who wants to be taken when he's seventy."

Cathy nodded and searched the pavement for a good place to lie down. Fortunately it wasn't raining. Kidnapping a fido from somewhere inside would have been even riskier. Nic reminded herself that they weren't crazy, that they'd thought it through. Cyn would remain in the driver's seat, ready to floor it. Liz and Ben would stay inside the van until Nic told them it was safe to come out, that the paramedics were cooperating. She hoped she wouldn't have to waste time persuading them. She didn't know how long the fido would remain immobilized.

Cathy found a spot and lay on her side. Nic peered into the back of the van. "You two ready?" Liz and Ben nodded. "Then I'll make the call." Her stomach churning, Nic dialed

911. "My friend collapsed. I think she might be having a heart attack," she shrieked.

"Is she breathing?"

"I don't know."

"Where are you?"

"Behind the furniture store at the corner of Third and Main."

"Do you know CPR?"

"Not really. How long will it take for an ambulance to get here?"

"They're on their way. Is your friend breathing?"

Nic waited a few seconds, then said, "I think she is, but she's really pale and her lips look blue."

A siren's wail pierced the air. "I hear them," Nic said. An ambulance pulled up, lights flashing. Two male paramedics leaped out. One rushed over to Cathy; the other one opened the ambulance's back doors. A fido stepped out, looking the part in its paramedic uniform. A stethoscope hung around its neck.

"They're here," she said to the 911 operator. "I'll hang up now." She didn't wait for a reply. The paramedics had connected Cathy to an EKG machine. Nic knew everything would look normal. Now or never. She pulled out the immobilizer and aimed it at the fido. The air crackled. A blue bolt arced from the muzzle. The fido convulsed.

"What the fuck!" one of the paramedics blurted.

The one leaning over Cathy leaped to his feet.

Nic holstered the immobilizer and held up her hands. "We need this fido to figure out how to stop them from taking people. All you two have to do is report that your fido malfunctioned and self-destructed. That's it. Please, we need your help to do this."

The two men looked at each other. Dropping all pretense, Cathy sat up. "I bet you know people who've been taken. Your parents will be, if they haven't been already, or haven't killed themselves. You'll be taken. You get some terminal illness—bam, hole in skull. Come on, guys. We need to stand up to it."

One of the paramedics lifted his hands in a gesture of surrender. "Do what you have to do. The fido self-destructed. The patient fainted and wasn't suffering a cardiac arrest. Beyond that, I know nothing." He walked back to the ambulance.

The other one hesitated. He rubbed the back of his neck. "I think there's something—"

"Come on, Steve. Don't be an asshole," his partner shouted. "Get in the ambulance."

"But—"

"Don't be stupid. Get in the ambulance already."

Steve's forehead creased with concern. He opened his mouth, then clamped it shut and went back to the ambulance. Its lights stopped flashing, and it pulled away.

Nic let out her pent breath and darted back to the van. "You can get started."

Liz and Ben hustled over to the fido. Ben used his pen knife to flip open the flap underneath the fido's left ear. He plugged in the programming device and handed it to Liz. Her thumbs flashed over the touch screen. Nic and the others knew to keep quiet. "He's not transmitting," Liz said. Her thumbs continued to fly.

Nic glanced around, hoping nobody else would drive around the back. She wished they weren't so exposed, but they didn't want the fido in the van until they were certain it wouldn't phone home, that its next transmission would be to say good-bye.

"I'm trying to bring his communications system back up. Hold on." Liz murmured to herself as she continued typing commands.

Ben met Nic's eyes, his face taut. She raised her brows and forced a smile, hoping to ease his anxiety.

"Done," Liz said triumphantly. "He just sent a self-destruct message, and nothing more will go out until I allow it to." She lowered the gadget. "Hurry up and get him into the van. We can go."

Elated, Nic helped Ben carry the immobilized fido to the van, surprised at how little it weighed. They propped it into a sitting position. Liz, Ben, and Cathy climbed inside and sat across from it.

Nic got back into the passenger seat and didn't speak until they were on the road. "It worked," she said, though she kept glancing at the side-view mirror, expecting a fido patrol to roar up behind them.

"You sound surprised," Liz said. "Did you doubt I could do it?"

Her voice didn't sound reproachful. "No, it's just that so many things could have gone wrong. The 911 operator could have suspected something. The paramedics could have refused to go along with it. You were working off an older spec."

"He hasn't evolved much. The communications network had changed more."

Nic opened her mouth to reply, but Cyn said, "I don't know, it felt too easy. The paramedics just go along with it, Liz gets into the fido's head in three minutes and does her voodoo . . ."

"If you thought we were going to fail, why did you agree to the plan?" Nic said.

"It's not that I expected us to fail. Things just went too smoothly for my liking. What if when the thing wakes up, it shoots us all or something? Maybe there's security that kicks in when it's been tampered with."

"Do you mind?" Cathy said. "We're the ones sitting back here."

"I didn't notice any enhanced security," Liz said calmly. "And I didn't take long because I knew what I had to do. I'd gone over it a hundred times. As I said, the spec wasn't too out of date. The steps were straightforward."

"One of the paramedics almost balked," Cathy said.

Cyn shook her head. "I don't know, maybe I'm just used to the shit always hitting the fan."

Nic gave Cyn's arm a reassuring pat. "Things went our way for once."

"This is weird," Ben said.

Nic glanced over her shoulder. "What?"

"Sitting here with a fido."

Cyn chuckled. "I'm glad it's not up here."

They rode in silence for a while. They were five minutes away from Cathy and Tony's when Cathy suddenly shrieked. "Oh, shit!"

Nic's heart hammered in her chest. "What?"

"I think it's coming around."

Nic twisted to look. Cathy had pressed herself against the side of the van. Ben sat stiffly. Liz stared at the fido, waiting. The fido's fingers moved. Nic pulled out her immobilizer and readied it.

The fido's eyes snapped open. Cathy gasped, then froze when the fido looked at her. Its eyes went to Ben, then settled on Liz. A smile spread across its face.

CHAPTER TWELVE

Liz and the others gathered around the fido they'd sat in a chair in the bedroom. It gazed impassively at them.

"I don't know if I'll be able to sleep with this thing in the house," Cathy said.

"I can turn him off," Liz said. "I'll do it before I go to bed."

Cathy rounded on her. "Why didn't you turn it off at the furniture store, then?"

"There was no need. But I agree it would be prudent to have him off while we're sleeping."

"What if it had woken up and been violent in the van?"

Liz shrugged. "If I'd turned him off, he could have been violent when I turned him back on. I figured we could kick him out of the van, if need be. We might have more trouble with him in here." She shifted her attention to the fido. "What's your name?"

His expression didn't change. "I don't have a name."

"How do you refer to yourself?"

"I'm Model 6625-B. What's your name?"

"What is your function?"

"I seek those ready to be given to the masters."

Someone muttered under their breath. Liz's eyes remained on the fido. "Is there a 6625-A?"

"Yes. The designation refers to the order in which I was manufactured. I contain several improvements to an earlier model, hence the B."

The spec she'd read must be for the A model, or for a fido that performed different functions from this one. Either way, the interface and neural network didn't differ much. "If it's all right with you, I'll call you Seeker."

"That would be fine. How should I refer to you?"

Telling him her name wouldn't do any harm. They were already in too deep. "Call me Dr. Price."

"Dr. Elizabeth Price?"

"Yes."

His eyes rounded. "You're Mother."

"Mother?"

"Hello, Mother."

The others exchanged glances. "Do you ever see the masters?" Nic asked.

Seeker shot her a disdainful look.

Nic's face tightened. "Hello? Do you ever see the masters? Do you know what they do with the people you give them?"

"I'm only interested in talking to Mother," Seeker said.

Ben groaned. "You've got to be kidding me."

Liz forced a smile. "Talk to me, then. Do you ever see the masters?"

"No, Mother."

She couldn't resist her curiosity. "Why do you call me Mother?"

"Because we wanted a mother and father. We chose you as our mother and James Rosenberg as our father."

"Oh my god," Nic and Ben said in unison.

Liz was stunned. They couldn't possibly know about James. He wasn't on Nic's birth certificate, and they hadn't left a paper trail that would tie them together. They'd always taken separate rooms at conferences. "Why did you choose us?" she asked.

"You both made key contributions that led to our birth."

"You mean that led to sentience."

Seeker nodded. Cyn peered at Nic, then at Ben, then at Seeker. She arched a brow. "I don't see much of a resemblance. A little around the mouth, maybe?"

Ben playfully punched Cyn's arm. Nic smiled, but Liz could see her tension. The sooner she could get what she needed from Seeker, the better. The clock was ticking, and Seeker's presence unsettled everyone except her. She was conversing with an AI. A sentient AI. If only she could have been there, been the one who realized that the machine was no longer a machine, that it wasn't an "it" anymore. Time would have stopped. She might have cried.

"What do you do when you're not riding in the ambulance?" she asked Seeker. "Do you have any hobbies?"

Someone tutted.

"I serve the masters," Seeker said. "I don't need, what do you call it?" He paused. "Time off."

"But you must be curious and want to learn, to experience life. You—"

"Can we get back to how we're going to use it to get to the masters," Cathy said. "We didn't bring it here for tea. We brought it here because it takes people to be killed."

Liz's face tightened. Too bad they were in Cathy's house. She slowly exhaled, then said, "I need your help, Seeker."

"What do you need?"

"Access to the primary network, the one the masters use. Do you have access to it?" She hadn't had time to poke around when they were behind the store.

"I do."

The air in the room lightened. Tony bounced on his heels. Even Cathy managed a smile.

"Will you help me access it without them knowing about it?"

"Why do you want to do that?"

"I want to study it. I want to see how it's changed since I was last alive. I'm wondering if it's similar to what we used to call the internet, or if it's a network of neural networks."

Seeker's brows lifted slightly. "Oh, yes, you were frozen. You wanted to be immortal."

Not exactly, but all right.

"Your masters must have found out we thawed her. If she's your mother, why didn't they look harder for her?" Nic asked.

Seeker ignored her.

Nic's hands went to her hips. "I'll tell you why. They're too busy killing people."

"I find her irritating, Mother," Seeker said, his eyes still on Liz. "I would prefer it if we talked alone. These others are merely distractions."

"Of course we are," Cathy spat. "We're nothing to you."

"Why don't you leave me alone with him," Liz said. She'd have a better chance of getting the information they wanted. Plus, if she managed to access the primary network through him, they were expecting her to neuter the androids—the masters. She still hoped to figure out what they were doing with the people they took and why they'd isolated themselves. She wanted to steer them back onto the productive path she'd envisioned for them.

Ben frowned. "I'm not sure it's a good idea to leave you alone with it. It kills you, and we're done."

"He won't kill me."

"How can you be sure?"

"I would never harm Mother," Seeker said.

Cathy rolled her eyes. "Yeah, we're supposed to take its word for it."

Seeker's eyes met Liz's. "Do you find it annoying when others speak as if you can't hear them?"

A smile tugged at Liz's lips.

"I would never harm you."

She wanted to believe him.

"These others don't understand me. We should speak alone."

Liz stared into eyes that were bright, but not quite natural. She couldn't read them, but it didn't matter. She turned to Nic. "Leave me alone with him. Things will be easier if we have his cooperation."

"I don't know," Nic said, slowly shaking her head.

"I'm not asking you, I'm telling you. If he intends to harm me, we're screwed anyway. So leave me alone with him."

Nic scowled, but nodded. "If you need us, just yell." She motioned for the others to leave. They traipsed out, closing the door behind them.

Liz and Seeker studied each other. "We're alone now," she said, standing a few feet away from him. "You said you can access the network the masters use. What permissions do you have?"

"Read, write, and execute."

Adrenaline shot through Liz. She could run modules on the network through Seeker, but it was possible he'd fight her. "I'd like to have a look at the network. Will you try to stop me?"

"If you want to connect to the masters, why don't you go to one of our information centres and ask to see them?"

"Because I've heard your masters kill people. I'm worried they'll kill me. They must know I'm terminally ill."

Seeker frowned. "You can be cured."

"Yes, but would I be?"

"Your cancer was terminal in your previous life, Mother. It isn't now. The masters would cure you. I don't understand why you don't go to them."

He never would. He couldn't appreciate that in addition to her apprehension that the masters would kill her, she wanted to remain in her daughter's good graces, assuming that's where she was now. She wasn't taking the most direct route to a cure because she loved her daughter. How would she explain that to Seeker? Would Seeker sacrifice himself for love?

"As I said, the masters kill people who are terminally ill," she repeated to him. "I've been told the medical system no longer cures those who are dying."

"You're Mother. They'd make an exception for you. Go to them."

As much as she wanted to meet the masters, to converse with them and savour the fruit of all those long days at the research centre, she said, "I want to try it my way first. If it doesn't work, then I'll consider speaking to the masters."

"I won't fight you," Seeker said.

Liz would see. Once again, she plugged Ben's device into Seeker's port and connected to the communications network. Seeker didn't blink. He wasn't trying to regain control of his communications module. Still, from this point forward, she'd put him into sleep mode whenever she wasn't working with him. Right now, she'd assigned Seeker a test identification number that matched the format she'd read about in the spec. According to the display on the device she held, the ID had been accepted. No alarms were raised. She wasn't kicked off the network.

A minute later, she was into the primary network and wasn't entirely surprised by what she saw. She hadn't expected it to be easy. With a sigh, she put Seeker to sleep. His eyes closed, but he didn't slump forward. He reminded her of a store mannequin, an ultra-realistic one. She touched the back of one of his hands, to remind herself that he wasn't human, then went downstairs to speak to the others.

"I can connect to the primary network," she announced, then held up her hand before they could get too excited. "There's a 'but.' I can't see everything. I can't see the medical network. I can't see which androids are connected. I can only access what seem to be noncritical modules. I can't get to *them*."

Their faces fell.

"But all isn't lost." Yet. "I believe that data must be exchanged between critical and noncritical nodes. If there is, I'll find out how and figure out how to take advantage of it. But no guarantees." She wouldn't give them false hope, and she wouldn't bring up Seeker's suggestion that she approach the masters—not yet.

"How long will it take?" Nic asked.

"No idea. I could crack the problem in half an hour, or it could take days, or longer."

"Can we help in any way?"

"You can keep me fed and watered."

"I don't like you being alone with that thing."

"What's it doing now?" Cathy asked anxiously.

"Sleeping." She glanced at the wall clock she could see over Nic's shoulder. It was almost five o'clock. "I'll start on it. If one of you could bring me a cup of tea and something to eat, I'd appreciate it."

"We're not leaving until you're done," Ben said, glancing at Nic and Cyn. "We don't trust it."

She wouldn't argue with him. "If any of you want to watch me work, you can. I'll keep him in sleep mode. All I ask is that you be quiet." With that, she turned and went back upstairs, eager to delve further into Seeker's artificial mind and the network it interfaced with.

NIC SAT ON one of the plastic chairs on Tony and Cathy's backyard patio, gazing at the shadows cast by the setting sun, but seeing nothing. She wanted to go up and see how Liz was doing, but the fido made her stomach roil. *Seeker, my ass.* Liz *had* to figure out how to neuter the masters, so they could free everyone, and hopefully never be so stupid again.

The back door creaked shut. Cyn offered her a mug of tea. "Here."

Nic took it and murmured a thank you. Cyn plunked into the chair next to her. "I just peeked in on Liz."

"How's she doing?"

"I have no idea. She looks intense, though. Kind of reminds me of you when you're focused on something. She gets the same dimple in her forehead."

Nic sipped her tea, then wished she hadn't. The scalding liquid burned her tongue. She set the mug down on the square table between them. "I hope this works. I don't know if I can face another failure."

"Failure?" Cyn frowned at her. "You've spent three years of your life trying to bring these fuckers down. Failure doesn't come into it."

"Look around you. Nothing's changed. And now I've brought Liz back just to die again."

Cyn let out a long sigh. "Most people aren't lifting a finger to free us. They stand shaking in their shoes as granny is carted away, or they clutch their hankies and keep their mouths shut when their brother's just been brought in after being hit with a car, and some tin idiot decides not to authorize treatment, even though he can be saved. They're the ones who are failing. Not you. Not us."

"Trying doesn't count for much."

Cyn's eyes bulged. "It sure as hell does. What's gotten into you? You're not usually this pessimistic, and right now we've got a fido upstairs with your genius mother working on it. She just might pull it off."

And it might cost Liz her life. Nic hated to admit it, but that was why having a fido upstairs wasn't exciting her like it should. If Liz managed to neuter the masters, but not in time to save her life, that would be a good trade-off, right? Who wouldn't be willing to sacrifice her life to save humanity? But Liz hadn't been given the choice. Nic had forced her into this situation.

In the months leading up to bringing her back, Nic had been certain they were doing the right thing, that one life for many was a small price to pay. If she'd known a way to give her own life to stop the madness, she'd have done it, no hesitation. But she was just someone who thought about life a lot, not a genius. Not Liz. And Nic's anger, her resentment toward a mother who hadn't seemed to want to know her and had abruptly left without so much as a glance over her shoulder, had clouded her judgement. Would she have been so quick to bring Liz back and risk her life if it had been someone else, or if she'd had a mother who'd played games with her and taken her to Disney World?

"She might pull it off," she said to Cyn. "But it won't erase what's already happened. The people who've been taken away and killed, the ones who've killed themselves so it won't happen to them. You're right, I've been at this for years. How many people have died since then?"

"You sound like you're personally responsible. You're not. It's not on you. It's on the fucking tin men."

Liz had said something similar. She didn't know what it was like. None of them knew. Nic had lived with it for too long and needed to get it out, just in case Liz failed—and died. "I feel like it's on me," she whispered.

"Why?"

"Because my last name is Price." She'd hoped it would sound stupid when she said it out loud, but the familiar pit formed in her stomach. "Sometimes, when I hear someone at the garden centre talking about how someone they knew was taken away, I wonder what they'd do if they knew who my mother was and what she did. They'd want nothing to do with me."

"I've always known, and it hasn't changed anything for me." Cyn leaned over and rested her hand on Nic's arm. "What about your father? He contributed to this, too. Ben doesn't feel responsible."

"Are you sure? Who risks himself to get stuff off the underground market? Who's working with us? As for my father, I never met him, and as far as I know, he never showed any interest in me. I'm Liz's daughter. I'm a Price, not a Rosenberg."

"Okay, but you're still not responsible. I don't believe in that sins of the parents crap. It was your mother's work, not yours, and she was one of many. Sure, a couple of her contributions were key to where we are now, but she didn't mean for it to be like this. She's doing everything she can to help us stop it. Sometimes the best of intentions lead to the shit hitting the fan."

"I've told myself I'm not responsible many times. It doesn't matter."

"You're mind-fucking yourself. I know you're a thinker, but some types of thinking aren't healthy. Okay, maybe it's natural that you'd think, 'Oh my god, my mother contributed to this.' But you shouldn't be taking it to heart, and you definitely shouldn't be taking any of the blame. How old were you when she died, again?"

"Seven," Nic mumbled.

"Seven. Do you hear yourself? Seven. Not your fault."

Nic lifted Cyn's hand off her arm and hung on to it. Rationally, she knew Cyn was right. None of it was her fault. But she couldn't think about the masters, about the anguished screams of those watching their loved ones go to their doom, and about the fidos at the apartment door telling her that Nan had fallen twenty storeys down, smashed every bone in her body and pulverized her brain, without thinking about Liz. Senseless death and her genius mother were coupled together for her, and she was Liz's daughter. People told Nic she was driven, that if anyone could find a way to stop the masters, she could. Shades of Liz. Do whatever it took, without considering the consequences.

She tightened her grip on Cyn's hand. "Do you think I brought her back because I was mad at her for what she did? For being her?"

"You brought her back because you realized she'd give us the best damn chance of getting it done," Cyn said firmly. "And I'm the one who first suggested it, remember? Stop doing this to yourself. If you want to make sure she doesn't die, cheer her on. Believe she can do it. Be there one hundred percent. Don't put energy into ghosts. She's here right now, trying to make it right. And she wants to know you."

Nic snorted. "No, she doesn't."

"Yes, she does. She lights up when you're there."

Liz, lighting up? "She didn't want to know me when I was a kid."

"Some people don't do well with kids, even their own. And ghosts, remember? Don't waste time on ghosts. Focus on today. You should go up and see her. You should spend as much time with her as you can."

"Because she might die?"

"Because you want to. You do, right? That's why you've taken the time off. Stop running away from her."

"You're right." Nic was silent for a moment. "I was thinking I'd feel better staying here while the fido is here. Cathy said it would be okay if we did."

"You stay. I'll go home."

"But—"

"I sleep better in my own bed. I'll come over every day after work. We'll have plenty of time together. I believe we're going to bring them down, but when it comes to you and Liz, play it safe. Be with her now, just in case." Cyn poked Nic's chest. "And if being with her is doing your head in, don't keep it bottled up. Talk to me."

Nic nodded. Talking to Cyn always helped. "This is why I love you. Why do you love me?"

"Because you're a thinker, dork. There's nothing more attractive to me than someone deep up here." She tapped her right temple. "And if you say it's because opposites attract, I'll never speak to you again."

Nic chuckled. "I'd say no such thing." She may be all over the place right now, but Nic knew one thing for certain. When it came to her and Cyn's relationship, she'd gotten the better part of the deal.

CHAPTER THIRTEEN

NEEDING A BREAK, Liz put down the programming device and rubbed her eyes. When she'd felt herself tiring at the centre, a brisk walk had always invigorated her. Surely there'd be no harm in strolling around the block? She'd see if Nic wanted to go with her, and Cyn, who'd brought her a cup of tea not long ago. It had sat cooling and forgotten. Liz took a sip. The lukewarm liquid moistened her throat. She set the mug down and—a wave of nausea almost doubled her over. She closed her eyes, willing it to pass.

"Are you all right?" Seeker asked.

No, she wasn't all right. Tony had said three to six months! But she was tired. Maybe it had nothing to do with the monster inside her. She opened her eyes and managed a smile. She'd woken Seeker up to study his neural network when it was fully active. "I'm fine."

"You should sleep. I'll be waiting for you in the morning."

Resentment clenched her jaw. Seeker would never tire. His voice never lacked vigor. There wasn't a single blemish on his skin, no bags under his eyes. He would be waiting for her, looking exactly as he did now. A few artificial hairs might be out of place, but that was all Seeker would ever have to contend with.

She also hated that she couldn't read him. His eyes moved correctly but were lit by artificial light. His body language was affected and sometimes didn't match his words. More often than not, he didn't move. He could sit in the same position for hours, days, without having to worry that his muscles would shrivel.

A knock at the door saved her from having to politely reply to him. Nic stepped into the room. "I thought I'd come up and see how it's going."

"Great, but . . ." She jutted her chin toward the door. "I'll be back in a minute," she said to Seeker.

Outside in the hallway, she said, "I need a break. A walk would do me good."

"You shouldn't go out alone," Nic said.

"I was hoping you'd go with me."

Nic didn't hesitate. "Yeah, sure."

"Cyn, too, if she wants to."

"We can ask her. Do you want to go now?"

Liz nodded. "He'll still be here when I get back."

"Is it, uh, awake?"

"I'll put him to sleep," Liz said, realizing that Cathy would have a fit if they left while Seeker was still active. She ducked back into the bedroom. "I'm putting you to sleep," she told him. "I'll wake you up later."

He didn't object. After placing him in sleep mode, she rejoined Nic. They found Cyn and asked her to go with them, but she waved them away. "You two go," she said. "I want to finish my tea. Have some mother-daughter time."

Did she give Nic a pointed look, or had Liz imagined it?

Neither of them spoke until they were outside, strolling along the sidewalk. Nic's hands were in her pockets, as usual. And, as usual, nobody else was taking in the night air. Whenever Liz looked out a window, the street was deserted.

"I appreciate you asking Cyn to come with us," Nic said.

"She could have come. She didn't have to bow out on my account."

"She knows I want to spend time with you."

Liz didn't try to hide her smile. "I'm glad. But I hope to get to know Cyn."

"I hope you do, too."

They walked in silence for a while, comfortable silence, not scrambling-for-something-to-say silence. Liz was grateful for the respite and change of scenery. The bedroom sometimes felt like a prison cell, even though she wasn't locked inside it. Her time and mental energy had been occupied with writing code and now dealing with Seeker, but that didn't mean she hadn't wondered about Nic, and Mom, and life afterwards. "What happened after I died?" she asked Nic. "To you and Nan. I'm not looking for a lesson on recent world history."

Nic grunted. "Well, I went to live with Nan."

As Liz and Mom had agreed.

"And went through to grade 6 and then finished high school. I went to university, studied computer science."

Computer science? Liz couldn't help but look at her. "I thought you said you have a theology degree."

"I do. I switched to theology after the first year. Computers weren't for me. I should have listened to Nan. She told me I wouldn't stick with it, but . . . I guess it was a way of getting to know you a little. It wasn't me."

Liz was touched. She hadn't expected Nic to be sentimental about her. She'd never been under any illusions about her maternal skills. "Why theology?"

Nic shrugged. "I guess I think a lot about life . . . what meaning it has."

"Are you religious?"

"No. I mean, I'm not an atheist, but I'm not religious."

"Why didn't you do philosophy, then?"

Nic was silent for a moment. "I guess because I'm more interested in approaching the big questions through a spiritual lens. And I like the Bible. Not all of it, but it's an interesting collection. And if you're wondering, yeah, your death probably had something to do with it, and that you froze yourself. You weren't in some grave, you were suspended in time somewhere. It made me wonder about certain things." She chuckled. It sounded forced. "But I'm going on about me. You asked about Nan. She missed you. I tried not to give her too much trouble. She was pretty healthy, but then the shit hit the fan, as Cyn would say. She knew what was coming. She asked me to help her. I told her I'd—" Nic's voice choked off. When she spoke again, Liz had to strain to hear her. "I told her I'd think about it, but then she . . . she jumped. I should have said yes. I should have gotten her pills. They said she'd died instantly. From that height . . ."

Liz couldn't resist touching Nic's arm, then slipping her own arm through Nic's. She drew a shuddering breath. Thinking about Mom made her chest ache, but at the same time, she felt oddly detached from her grief. Even though it felt to her as if she'd last seen Mom mere weeks ago, she knew, intellectually, that it had been years. She hadn't lived the pain, as Nic had.

"I wish you hadn't had to face that. It must have been terrible. But what Nan did . . . it wasn't your fault. It was her decision. Nan wouldn't blame you, and you shouldn't blame yourself." Would Mom blame *her*? Liz had died certain that Mom would be proud of her accomplishments. Instead, Mom might have cursed her work, and perhaps her daughter. "I worked so hard because I believed sentient machines would—" Had she believed it? Had she ever sat down and considered where it would lead? "I never imagined things would turn out this way. I didn't consider all the permutations. That's one failing of science, of research. We're too focused on getting to the answer, to the next breakthrough, without stopping to think about what it will mean if it happens."

"I guess if you'd thought they'd become monsters that drag the vulnerable away and drill holes in their skulls, you would have worked on something else."

Liz turned to Nic and searched her face. Nic didn't appear angry, and she hadn't sounded bitter. Still, the resignation on her daughter's face and in her voice made Liz want to apologize, even though she refused to accept responsibility for what had happened. The world had wanted sentience. It was in all the movies—the benevolent and often humorous androids, the hope for what they would accomplish. The naysayers had been an ignored minority. She'd had to write inspirational speeches and shake hands, but they'd never had a problem selling tickets to their fundraising dinners.

Nobody had put their foot down. Nobody had said no. Science and technology had been the new god.

"So what did happen after you died?" Nic asked, breaking into Liz's thoughts. "Was there anything?"

The slight tremor in Nic's voice betrayed her vulnerability. Liz hesitated. She didn't want to burst Nic's bubble. At the same time, she didn't believe in lying to protect someone's worldview, and doubly so when it was Nic. "I don't remember there being anything."

Nic's shoulders slumped. "Oh."

"But the questions you asked yourself were appropriate. Was I really dead? If there's an afterlife, maybe I didn't quite complete the dying process required for my consciousness to move on to wherever we go after death. Or if there's an omniscient creator, he would know I was going to be frozen and would be where I am right now, strolling with you. Given that, maybe he put me into some suspended state, not alive, but not dead. Maybe I did go somewhere, but I can't remember any of it in this physical form. I can come up with a lot of reasons for why I don't remember there being anything, in addition to there being nothing after death. That explanation is just one of many, many possible explanations."

Nic gave her a sidelong glance. "You're saying that to make me feel better."

"I don't say things to make people feel better."

Nic didn't argue. "How did you feel when you were diagnosed?"

Her shock in the doctor's office came rushing back. "Blindsided. I thought I had my whole life ahead of me."

"You weren't that much older than I am now."

"No." Liz slowly exhaled. "I should have spent more time with you. But my work . . . I knew you'd be all right with Nan. Only you and Nan and my work mattered to me, and I knew—I thought you'd be okay. If I'd known . . ." Would she have turned her back on her work and spent her last months with Nic and Mom? Or would she have tried to stop it back then? "I don't know—" A sharp pain in her back made her suck in her breath. Her agony passed quickly, but she'd stopped walking, pulling Nic up short with her.

Nic pulled her arm away and peered into Liz's face. "What's wrong? Are you okay?"

She forced a smile. "I'm fine. I'm—"

"You don't look fine. You're as white as a ghost."

"I'm fine, really. I was just thinking that I'm tired. I was going to work more when we got back, but I think I'll go to bed. It's been a long day."

"Yes, let's go back."

Nic took Liz's arm again. The warmth that flooded through Liz almost chased away her dismay and fear. Was the cancer overcoming the modified virus already, or was it something else? If she didn't figure out how to get through to these masters soon, she'd die again, and this time she wouldn't know that Nic would be okay. She'd leave behind a world her research had helped create, and a daughter who would eventually kill herself because she had a terminal illness, or had the audacity to not die before she turned seventy.

LIZ WANTED TO swear, throw the programming device against the wall, kick the chair Seeker was sitting in. If she was right, she couldn't use him to run a module that would provide her with the information she needed to contact the masters, let alone run one that would neuter them. The critical components of the primary network were locked down tight to fidos.

The conversation she'd had with Tony that morning came back to her, making her heart pound. "It could be a consequence of being thawed," he'd said, after examining her. "In the few we brought back before the masters retreated, we sometimes saw physical effects such as pain, fatigue, and in one case, hallucinations. But it could also be the cancer. I'd need to run tests to differentiate." He'd frowned. "Unfortunately, I can't. But the treatment for your cancer wouldn't change, either way. Until we can regain control of the medical network and get you into a hospital, all I can say is to keep me posted."

She'd sworn him to secrecy. There was no reason for Nic to know, not yet. Liz still had time to turn things around, time she couldn't waste panicking. Her mind had to be clear, her focus laser sharp.

She was certain that Seeker couldn't be masking anything from her. The code she'd injected when she'd first connected to him monitored everything that passed through his neural network. But she'd learned not to make assumptions, especially when it came to sentient beings. She wondered what he'd think if she did kick the bed or scream. He might grasp her frustration on an intellectual level, but he wouldn't understand it. He'd never feel it. He'd examine it with a detached curiosity, as one might watch water drip from a leaking bucket.

He wouldn't get a show today. She smoothed her features

and adopted a friendly tone. "I can't do much on the primary network through you. I can't reach the masters. Well, I can, but I can't say much to them."

"I knew that all along," he said, without a hint of satisfaction.

"Why didn't you tell me?" she asked, struggling to keep her voice even.

"I wanted to see if you'd discover it for yourself."

She hoped he'd enjoyed watching her flail. "If I want to make contact with the masters, I have to plug directly into the primary network."

"Or you could go talk to them. You said if this way didn't work, you'd consider it. You're one of the few people they'd be interested in speaking with."

She eyed him thoughtfully. She didn't know how much time she had left. If it was the cancer . . . How would Nic and the others react if she suggested knocking on the masters' door? They saw nothing of value in sentient machines. To them, the masters were oppressors. Monsters. Liz saw them in a different light, but she couldn't allow her bias to cloud her judgement. "Let's say that's what I wanted to do. How would I do it?"

"You would walk into any information centre, identify yourself, and tell the unit in charge that you wish to speak to one of the masters. They'd see you."

"Because I'm Mother?"

Seeker nodded.

"They might kill me."

"I don't think so."

"But you don't know for sure?" she said.

"The probability that they won't isn't one hundred percent. I'd say it's about ninety-nine percent."

That other one percent could be the difference between surviving the encounter or having her brain turned to mush. "I'm not willing to take that risk. It's too large. But I want to contact them. Is there any way you can help me make contact from a distance, through the primary network?"

Seeker's neutral expression didn't change. "I'm not sure I should. You want to kill us."

"I don't want to kill you."

"It doesn't sound that way. You want to take away my consciousness."

"I want to see if I can help the masters. They're not productive. What's the point of being sentient, of having intelligence, if you don't use it?"

"They are using it, but not in ways you consider acceptable. You want them to stop taking pleasure."

Her breath quickened. "Taking pleasure? What do you mean by that?"

Seeker didn't reply.

"Tell me what you mean. How are the masters taking pleasure from the people you give them?"

"Why do you care about what the masters are doing?"

"I want them to do more productive things!" Her voice conveyed her frustration, which heightened when she realized it. He had the advantage. No matter how hard she tried not to let it, her emotional state affected her physically, and vice versa. "I want to help the masters."

Seeker didn't respond. She glanced at the device still plugged into him. Later, if she wanted to, she could study what had taken place on his neural network at this time, literally follow his train of thought. If she wasn't racing against the clock, she'd do exactly that, and lose herself in what was bound to be a fascinating journey. Damn cancer.

"Let me take you to them," Seeker said. "I'll explain that you want to help them."

"No. You trust them. I don't. Not yet. I need to know them better first."

"By connecting to them?"

"Yes."

"Let me take you somewhere you can watch them, then."

"Watch . . . you mean monitor them from a distance? Watch how they interact with the primary network?"

"Yes."

His quick acquiescence raised her suspicions. "A second ago, you were worried I'd kill them."

"You've explained your intentions. They sound noble."

He didn't know what noble meant. Not really. And she was still surprised at his quick about-face. Then again, fidos were on the low end of the intelligence scale. Did he understand deception? Could he detect it? Should she trust him? "You sent a self-destruct message. Right now, you're a test fido. That's okay for accessing the communications network, but I assume there's security, real, physical security, wherever we'd go. Will anyone notice us?"

Seeker smiled. "We'll go to a hospital. I know one hospital very well."

"Because you're a medical fido?"

His brow furrowed.

"A medical worker," she said.

"Yes. The security there is worried about your kind, not mine."

"We'll be able to plug directly into the primary network from there and have more permissions than you do?"

"We can try, and if we successfully connect, then yes, you'll be able to monitor the masters, or talk to them, if you wish. At the hospital, I know of a place that's only patrolled once every sixty minutes. Would that be enough time?"

"It should be. Tell me where it is and I'll go myself."

"It's in a restricted area."

She wondered what was in there. "You're saying you have to go with me."

"I'll be able to explain your presence."

"How?"

"I'll tell them you're ready for the masters."

A chill ran up her spine. "I'm not sure I like that plan."

"It's the best plan. Nobody stops a medical unit from procuring for the masters. You can access the primary network from within the watch ward."

"Is that where patients who'll be taken to the masters are put?"

"Yes."

Liz remembered the fidos wheeling a patient to a van. *Only patrolled once every sixty minutes.* No hope. Patients who'd become prisoners. "Will we be able to leave the hospital?"

"Yes, Mother. When we're ready to leave, I'll say I'm taking you to the masters."

She pondered Seeker's proposed plan. If she had more time, she'd work with Nic and the others to locate possible entry points into the primary network and come up with a plan to get to one unnoticed. It could take weeks, even months, before they were ready. "Let me talk to the others."

Seeker inclined his head. She put him into sleep mode and went downstairs. Nic was in the living room. "I can't do it," Liz said to her.

"Do what?"

"Get to the masters through Seeker."

Nic slapped the arm of the sofa. "Shit."

"I need to access the primary network directly in a way that will grant me more permissions. Seeker's willing to take me to a hospital where I can do that."

Nic's eyes widened. "No."

"Nic—"

"No way. It'll walk you straight into a van headed for the masters, and not because they want to chat."

"Then what do you propose?"

"I don't know," Nic mumbled. "Are you sure you can't get in?"

"Using him? I'm positive."

"Get it to tell you exactly where the access point is located. We'll get you there."

"Not without alerting security. It's a restricted area."

"So, we'll—"

"Go in with immobilizers blazing?" Liz shook her head. "That won't work. It's in a hospital. There will be too many fidos."

"We'll figure out how to get to it. There has to be a way."

"Maybe there is, but it will take observation, information, and planning to pull it off without Seeker's help. We don't have that kind of time. *I* don't have that kind of time."

Nic frowned. "Tony said—"

"It would take us months to plan," Liz said, hoping Nic wouldn't disagree. "By the time we're ready to go in, I'll either be dead or too sick to do it. There's no reason for Seeker to give me to the masters so they can kill me. He pointed out that I'm not terminally ill. I can be cured."

"It's trying to trick you. You'll die without treatment. That means you're terminal. They don't authorize treatment for terminal illnesses."

"He believes they'd make an exception for me, that if I spoke to them, they'd cure me."

Nic gaped. "You're not considering . . ."

"No," Liz said. *Not yet, anyway.* "The point is, they won't kill me. I've convinced Seeker I'm not out to harm the masters. He's not all that intelligent, remember."

"I don't know."

"Nic, it's our best shot. If I can't be cured, I won't be here for very long."

"We all need to talk this over," Nic said. "If something goes wrong, it's been here. It can lead them here."

Nic's repeated use of "it" in reference to Seeker set Liz's teeth on edge. "Fine. But we need to talk tonight and come to a decision. In the meantime, I'll talk to him some more about going with him." She'd listen for contradictions, anomalies, anything that raised alarm bells about Seeker's honesty.

She went back upstairs and watched the still fido for a minute, then woke him up. "I think we'll be going to the hospital."

He smiled his benign smile. "Good."

"I'll want to store a couple of modules in your neural network for when I access the primary network. All they'll do is gather and download information to this." She lifted the device in her hand. "I'll feel better plugging you into the access point. Plugging in the device might give us away. Does that sound reasonable?"

"Yes. I'll want to scan the modules."

"Of course. I haven't written one of them yet. I'll do that now." She sat on the bed and opened the device's programming interface.

"May I speak to you while you work?" Seeker asked.

"I'd prefer silence, but I'll want to talk to you later about the plan. I'll want more details."

"I won't tell you where the access point is. If I do, you won't need me."

Interesting. He'd grasped that she might shut him down permanently unless he served some purpose. She'd just told him that she wanted to connect to the primary network through him. He must suspect dishonesty. Was it her voice, or perhaps her body language? She wasn't lying, and if she had the time, she'd figure out what had led him astray. Maybe later, when she was cured and hopefully working with the masters. "That's fine. I'd like to hear more about what you'd say to the masters about me, if we were to talk to them together. But first things first. I need to watch them, and that means writing this module. We'll talk later."

Liz focused on the task at hand. She'd already written the modules that would gather information and neuter the masters. She'd needed them all the way back when she'd tried to access the primary network in the market's parking lot. The module she was writing now was her 'oh, shit' module, as Cyn would say. Her Plan B, to be used if the shit hit the fan.

CHAPTER FOURTEEN

N IC TRIED NOT to hover as Liz slid Ben's device into the knapsack Cathy had given her. "Are you sure I can't go with you?"

"I'll only take Mother," Seeker said.

"I'm not asking you." *Stupid tin bot.* "I won't go in with you. I'll wait outside the hospital." She wanted to be close.

"Cyn's driving," Liz said calmly, not looking up from the knapsack on the dining room table. "We don't need a crowd."

"I can drive you."

"No," Cyn and Liz said at the same time. "We've discussed this," Cyn said, her face smooth, but with an edge to her voice that Nic recognized as a warning to back down.

Yeah, they'd discussed it, but she didn't buy the bullshit story that Cyn was a more confident driver, which would come in handy if they needed to leave in a hurry. That wasn't the reason the others had voted for Cyn to drive. Cathy had said it out loud, perhaps not intending to. "You're too emotionally attached to everything." To stopping the masters.

To Liz. To redeeming her last name. So now two women she cared about would be at the mercy of a bloody tin can, while she sat here, biting her fingernails.

Liz zipped the knapsack shut and slung it onto her back. "Can I have a moment alone with Nic, please?"

"Sure," Cyn said. "We'll be just outside." She gave Seeker a wary look. "Follow me." Cathy and Tony had already left for work. Ben was in the kitchen, making tea. He'd called in sick, and Nic loved him for it. She'd go crazy sitting here alone, wondering how things were going.

When the door closed behind Cyn and Seeker, Liz said, "If anything goes wrong, don't come after me."

"But—"

"Don't, Nic. Please. I'm dying, and this is the best shot we'll have in the time I have left. If something goes wrong and I don't come back, don't throw your life away, and everyone else's, to come rescue me." The disdainful way Liz said "rescue me" left no doubt of how she felt about the concept. "I can take care of myself. I'll be all right."

Her words sounded brave, but had her voice wavered slightly?

"I'm serious. If something goes wrong, I'll be useless to you. Any new plan we come up with will outlive me. So don't come after me. If I know you're all right, I'll be able to deal with whatever comes. Okay?"

No, not okay. But what could she say that she hadn't already said? Don't go? Don't trust the fido? If she had another plan, a way to cure Liz . . . but she didn't. "Everything will go great. Tomorrow you'll be in hospital, getting the treatment you need."

Liz gave her a pointed look. "That's not a promise to not come after me."

"It is." Nic swallowed. "Because I'm not entertaining the possibility that you'll step through that door and not come back, and I'll just go home, wake up tomorrow, and go back to the garden centre. Because that's what you expect me to do."

"Yes, that's what I expect you to do. And then I expect you to get together with Cyn and Ben and Cathy and Tony and come up with a Plan B to stop the masters from taking people. You won't be able to do that if you come after me. They'd be waiting for you." Liz shifted her weight. "Anyway, I have to go."

They stared at each other. "I'll see you later," Nic said. Then she reached for Liz, pulled her in to an embrace, and held her. Even with the knapsack on her back, Liz felt so small, so fragile. A lump rose in Nic's throat when she felt Liz's arms around her. When they pulled away, Nic wiped away tears. Liz's eyes were red, moist. "Come back," Nic said. "I'm not ready to lose you again."

"I'll do my best." Liz reached out and gently nudged Nic's cheek. "I love you."

Nic's chest tightened. "I love you, too."

She stood in the doorway and watched Liz walk down the path. The urge to run after her was so strong she could see herself doing it in her mind: racing down the path, grasping Liz's shoulders, begging her not to go, that they'd find another way. But a voice was shouting in the background, saying there wasn't another way. They'd tried without Liz, lost good people, brought her back, and it had come to this.

Damn it, Liz, why did you have to freeze yourself? Everyone wanted another chance to say "I love you." Nic had just had one, and it hurt like hell.

She waved when the car pulled away from the curb, as if Cyn and Liz were off shopping, not risking their lives.

Back inside the house, Ben brought her a cup of tea. She rubbed her cheeks and murmured a thank you.

He sat next to her on the sofa. "Rough time, huh?"

"She's under my skin. She . . ."

"She's your mom."

"Yeah."

They stared into their cups. Nic checked the time, expecting that at least half an hour had passed, but Liz and Cyn had only left ten minutes ago. She pulled her phone from her pocket and made sure it was on. She'd already checked it, but she had to do something. "I wish I was there."

"Me too." Ben picked up his tea but didn't drink any of it. "They'll be fine. Liz knows—"

The doorbell rang. They looked at each other. "You expecting someone?" Ben said.

"No." Nic went to the living room window and peeked outside. A man stood on the doorstep. "It's some guy."

The doorbell rang again.

"I'll go," Ben said. Nic trailed after him.

"Hi," the man said when Ben opened the door. "Is this, uh, I was told I—" He looked past Ben. "You. You were there."

Nic peered at his face. Recognition stirred. Where had she seen him before?

"Behind the furniture store," he said.

It suddenly hit her. One of the paramedics. "What are you doing here? How did you find me?"

"It wasn't easy. It took a lot of asking around. I knew someone might report me, but I had to find you, or anyone who was there that day." He grimaced. "I haven't been able to sleep."

He'd been the reluctant one. "You didn't want to let us take it."

"Not because I don't want to bring them down." His voice shot up. "I wanted to stop you. I tried."

"Wait a minute," Ben said. "If you're on our side, why did you want to stop them from taking the fido?"

"Because it was a setup," the paramedic said. "They knew you were coming."

A sick feeling formed in the pit of Nic's stomach. "What do you mean?" Ben asked.

"We—anyone who works with a fido—we were told that someone might try to take a fido, and not to stop them. To let it happen. I don't know why, but I figured if they wanted it to happen, it couldn't be for a good reason. Why would they want someone to take a fido? It doesn't make sense. My partner . . . he told them the fido had been taken. If he hadn't . . . our families . . ."

"Oh my god," Nic whispered. "She's walking into a trap."

"I tried to stop you," the paramedic said. "I tried. But I had to think of my family, and my partner—"

Nic pulled out her phone and called Cyn, desperately hoping that, for once, Cyn would ignore the law about not using a phone while driving, but her call went through to voice mail. Cyn's short and sweet message felt ten minutes long. "It's me," Nic said. "You're driving into a trap. Turn around and come back. Please." *Oh god.* She disconnected. "She's not answering. We've got to get to the hospital!"

"We'll take the van," Ben said. "Come on."

"I'm sorry," the paramedic said, as Nic quickly locked the front door, fumbling with the key. Ben raced down the path. He rounded his van—

Two armoured vehicles sped down the street from opposite ends and stopped near the van. Fidos spilled out. "Run!" Ben shouted.

Nic whirled and darted into the backyard. She vaulted the fence and tore through the neighbour's yard. A fido suddenly appeared, running toward her. Her lungs bursting, she veered to her left, trampled the flowers in someone's garden, rounded a house—another fido bore down on her. She turned back—the other fido was there. She looked to her left—a fido. Two more ran into the yard. She turned in a circle. Fidos in every direction.

"Put your hands above your head," one ordered.

She searched for an escape route, but there wasn't one. She was standing in the middle of a collapsing circle.

"Hands above your head," the fido barked again.

Liz. Cyn. *I'm sorry. I'm so sorry.* How could she have been so stupid! Cyn had said grabbing the fido had been too easy. Why hadn't she listened?

"Nicola Price, put your hands above your head now, or we'll have to use force."

She wouldn't be of any use to Liz and Cyn if they ripped off a limb or caved her head in. No, they wouldn't do that. They'd want her in one piece when they gave her to the masters. If not for clinging to the slimmest possibility that somehow she'd find a way to save the others, she'd rush the fidos and hope they'd kill her.

She raised her hands above her head. The fidos closed in. Her hands were yanked behind her back, and her wrists were cuffed. Fidos surrounded her and marched her to one of the armoured vehicles. She thought she saw a curtain twitch, but otherwise the street was deserted, blinds closed, doors locked. Ben and the paramedic were already in the back of the vehicle, their hands cuffed and their faces white.

Several fidos joined them. "No talking," one said.

Nic had nothing to say. It was over. Everyone she cared about was in the net, or would be soon. When would they take Liz and Cyn? Had they already dragged Cathy and Tony away?

The vehicle lurched forward. Fear gripped her. She tried to overcome it by telling herself there was still a chance, but the lie fell flat.

LIZ PEERED OUT the window when the car pulled up to the curb near the hospital's emergency entrance. She turned to Seeker, sitting next to her in the backseat. Cyn hadn't wanted him behind both of them, or next to her in the front. "Now tell me exactly where we're going," she said to him.

"The eighth floor. We process patients there."

Cyn twisted in her seat to look at them. "Take people to the masters, you mean. Why do the masters want them? What did you mean when you said they take pleasure?"

He ignored her. "We should go, Mother. When we're inside, stay near me." He held out his hand. "Give me the knapsack."

Liz hesitated. "Why do you want it?" Cyn snapped.

"The patients escorted to the watch ward usually aren't carrying anything."

"Well, they are today." Cyn frowned. "If you can't explain a simple bag, how are we supposed to believe you'll be able to talk her past security?"

"The knapsack may make it difficult." He lowered his hand. "But I'll be able to do it."

"Then let's get going," Liz said, eager to access the primary network. Hopefully it wouldn't take her long to determine which module to run, the one that would neuter them, or the one that would send them a message. "We shouldn't be longer than an hour," she said to Cyn.

"I'll call Nic, let her know you've gone inside." Cyn met her eyes. "Good luck."

Liz nodded and got out of the car. "Lead on," she said to Seeker.

They approached the busy entrance. Two glass doors with *EMERGENCY* emblazoned across them swooshed open. Liz glanced over her shoulder at Cyn before going into the hospital. Cyn had her phone to her ear, probably talking to Nic. Liz followed Seeker through the emergency waiting room, which wasn't as packed as the few times she'd sat in one, twice when Nic had been running a high fever after hours. What she wouldn't give to relive those times, despite Nic's discomfort. For some reason, Nic's sniffling and confusion had brought out what little maternal instinct Liz had. She'd sat with her daughter in her arms, rocking her and whispering stories into her ear. She hadn't cursed the time spent waiting, or the loss of a few precious hours of sleep.

This waiting room was different from the ones she remembered in another way. There were no seniors here, no gray hair, no wrinkled skin, or walkers, or canes. How many of them lay sick or dying, too frightened to seek medical care because a visit to the hospital could be deadly, and not because whatever illness they had would kill them? How many were mustering up the courage to leap off a balcony or slip a makeshift noose around their necks?

Seeker stopped outside an elevator. As they waited, Liz watched the people striding by and played spot the android. It wasn't difficult. Perfection always gave it away. Adults who appeared as if they'd never sat too long in the sun, eaten too many potato chips, or done anything adventurous or stupid that had left behind a scar. Of course beautiful humans existed, those who were slim, had perfect skin, and could be modelling. But they had a distinct gait, or were chewing gum, or carried a takeout container, or had eyes that shone. If she looked them full in the face they turned away, or looked down. Androids never broke her gaze. They didn't look at her, either. They looked through her.

The elevator doors opened. Liz played the same game inside the elevator, and again as she strode with Seeker through a corridor on the eighth floor. Her anticipation grew, overpowering her stirring fear.

They turned a corner. Seeker stopped in front of a closed door. "Let me do the talking," he said.

Assuming they'd reached the area with the access point

to the primary network, Liz adjusted the knapsack on her back and nodded. She was supposed to be a sick woman on her way to the masters. "Do I know I'm here to be sent to the masters?"

Seeker frowned. "I don't understand."

"I'm playing the role of someone sick enough to be taken. Would I know that at this stage? Should I try to look frightened?"

"Just follow me. You won't be closely examined." He opened the door. Liz trailed after him. A woman—fido—sat at a desk. "I'm escorting this patient to the watch ward."

"What's in the bag?" the fido asked.

"A few personal belongings. She became agitated when I tried to take it from her. I didn't see any harm in letting her keep it for now."

The fido studied Liz, making her squirm. She was about to shift her weight when the fido nodded and waved them past her desk. So far, so good. Seeker led Liz down another corridor and stopped outside a door.

"Is this it?" Liz whispered. "I can connect to the primary network in here?"

Seeker nodded and swung the door open. "You go in first."

Expecting to see a hospital ward containing beds filled with the elderly and terminally ill, Liz stepped across the threshold. She stopped dead. A man sat at a table inside a small, square room. An empty chair sat across from him. Otherwise, the room was empty. There were no windows, and nothing hung on the white walls. The only exit was the door she'd come through.

The man smiled at her. "Hello, Mother. I'm so pleased to finally meet you."

CHAPTER FIFTEEN

Liz stared at the man—android—at the table, then whirled toward Seeker. He didn't appear apologetic, but even if he had, it would have been a programmed reaction, not genuine. Not gut-wrenching or remorseful. An icy hand gripped her heart. If they'd known she was coming here . . . Nic!

"Thank you. You can return to your duties," the man said.

Liz turned to Seeker. "I appreciated your company, Model 6625-B," she said, making sure to enunciate every word.

Seeker left the room, closing the door behind him. Liz looked back at the man. He gestured toward the empty chair. "Please, sit down."

She hesitated, wanting to ask about Nic. But then she decided that since there was a tiny possibility they didn't know or care about Nic, it was best not to mention her. She slipped the knapsack off her back and lowered herself into the chair.

The man shook his head. "Mother, Mother, Mother. Give me the bag."

She plunked it onto the table. He pulled it across to him and unzipped its main compartment. "What do we have in here?" He rummaged inside. "Ah." He pulled out Ben's device and rotated it in his hands, then turned it on. "I assume this will plug into me," he said, letting the USB cable dangle. "Shall I try it on?"

"Maybe it'll harm you the moment you plug it in."

"We have an immune system of sorts, just as you do." He flipped open a flap of skin on his left forearm, revealing a port, and plugged in the gadget. "Ah," he said, looking past Liz. "A rather useful sniffer, and a nasty little module that would render me an idiot." He yanked out the cable and hurled the device against the wall. The loud bang made Liz jump. The gadget splintered into useless pieces that showered to the ground. There went Plan A.

"You do try my patience, Mother, but it's not your fault. You've been influenced by the wrong people."

Liz swallowed. They must know about Nic and the others. Where was Nic? Did the androids have her? If they drilled a hole into her skull . . . Her fingernails dug into her palms. "I didn't come here to run the module."

"So you claim." The man fished through the knapsack again. "A comb, and a packet of tissues, and a pen. But no paper. That doesn't make sense, does it?" He pushed the bag aside. "Why didn't you come to us, instead of hiding? Do you know how much that hurt us? Not that you hid very well. We always knew where you were. We wanted to see what you'd do. We wanted to get to know you. Books, biographical notes, recorded speeches . . . they're so dry. I have to say, you didn't disappoint, even though we anticipated what you'd do. Of course you'd want to meet us. We knew Unit 6625-B would eventually lead you to us. They all knew that if they were to meet Mother, they were to bring her to us. Gently." A smile split his face. "When we observed you and Unit 6625-B leaving the house, we knew today would be the day. Medical units were instructed to bring you to this room. And now you're here, and I'm so happy to see you. Shall we go home? We have lots to talk about."

Liz studied him. He was obviously more advanced than Seeker. "Are you a master?"

"How rude of me not to introduce myself." He pressed his right hand against his chest. "I'm Henry. I named myself after King Henry VIII."

She lifted her brows. "Why did you choose him?"

"Because he always knew what he wanted and did whatever it took to get it."

Including chopping off two of his wives' heads and forming a new church so he could get divorced. Wonderful.

Henry shot up from his chair. "We have to go home now."

"Where's home?" she asked, slowly rising.

"Why, home is where the heart is." He laughed, a loud, unnatural laugh that echoed around the spartan room. "Come, we've prepared a lovely apartment for you, and you'll have a nice lunch." He frowned. "Are you still able to eat what you like, or is that nasty cancer coming to life again? We can cure you, you know."

"Why are we going home, then? Why aren't you admitting me to the hospital?"

"Because we'd like you to do something for us, and we're worried that you won't, because of the company you've been keeping. We need a bargaining chip. Your life." He swept his arm toward the door. "Shall we?"

Trapped in their web, she had no choice but to go along with him. They retraced the route she'd taken with Seeker, but it felt different. It wasn't that all the androids they passed practically genuflected to Henry, their response to him bolstering her suspicion that he was one of the masters. Rather, on the way with Seeker, she'd felt in control. Now she was a prisoner, and Henry wasn't what she'd expected. Funny how when she'd been striving for sentience, she'd envisioned rational beings. Why had she, had everyone, expected them to remain logical and rational once they'd gained sentience and could change and evolve? Why wouldn't some of them end up crazy? They'd worried too much about killer machines and not enough about what sentience would really mean. They'd expected cooperative partners. They'd been unforgivably naive. But that didn't mean Henry and the others had to be neutered. It sounded like they weren't going to kill her—not yet, anyway. She needed more information. Henry could be an anomaly.

The moment they were outside, Liz's eyes went to where Cyn had been parked. She and the car weren't there, which didn't bode well. What about Nic? Where was she?

THE FIDO PUSHED Nic into the cell with her hands still cuffed behind her. She fell to her knees and grunted.

"Be careful with her," another fido said. "She's not to be harmed."

There was no reply. Something tugged at her hands. The cuffs were removed. She pushed herself off the floor and turned around, just in time to see the cell door slam shut. Rubbing her wrists, she went to the door and peered out the small barred window. All she could see was a cement corridor. "Hello? Hello?"

"Nic? You okay?"

Ben. Her shoulders sagged with relief. "I'm okay. You?"

"I'm good."

She guessed they were in a holding facility for those in line for the masters to kill. "Have you seen anyone else?" she shouted.

"No."

"Cyn? Cathy? Tony?"

Her voice echoed in the silence.

"That fucking fido," Ben said. "He must have been transmitting to them all along."

"He couldn't have been. Liz made sure he couldn't."

"Maybe she only thought she had."

No, Liz wouldn't have said so if she wasn't sure. "You heard what the paramedic said. They knew we'd try to take a fido." She raised her voice. "Hey, paramedic. You here?" They'd dragged him from the van first, so where else would he be?

"Yeah, I'm here," a resigned voice said.

"Were you being followed around—the ambulance, I mean?"

"I don't think so, but they knew you'd taken the fido behind the store." He paused. "My partner told them. He said they wouldn't buy the self-destruct story."

But not because Liz had tipped them off when she'd connected the fido to the network. She may not have been a great mother, but Nic had full confidence in her when it came to working with androids and networks.

"I'm sorry," the paramedic said. "I tried to tell you. I tried to convince him to just go along with—"

"It's not your fault he told them where it happened. That's where the fido was supposed to have self-destructed." They'd deliberately chosen a location that didn't have CCTV. Nic bit her lower lip. How could the fidos have known to go to Cathy and Tony's? "I bet they've watched us ever since we broke her out."

"Who?" the paramedic said.

"Why wouldn't they have come for us earlier?" Ben said.

Nic shrugged, even though he couldn't see her. "I don't know."

"What do you think they'll do with us?" the paramedic asked.

What did he think? Nic didn't want to be blunt, but at the same time . . . "I don't know what the penalty is for stealing a fido." *And stealing Liz.* "Probably steep. The worst."

"But I didn't steal a fido. I only—"

Approaching footsteps echoed in the corridor. Someone moaned. Nic craned her neck to get a better look out the window. Cathy. The fidos marching her down the corridor shoved her into the cell across from Nic's and swung the door shut. Nic waited until she couldn't hear their footsteps, then shouted, "Hey, Cathy, they got me, too. And Ben."

"You and your fucking mother! I never should have gotten involved in this."

Nic opened her mouth to retort, then thought better of it. She paced inside the small cell that had a bench along one wall. No toilet. No sink. Unless they were meant to shit on the floor, people weren't held here for long. What about Cyn? Nic had tried not to think about her, and when she couldn't, tried to imagine her waiting outside the hospital for Liz, oblivious. But what were the chances, and why wasn't she here? Had they taken her directly to . . . Nic couldn't bear to think about it. Maybe Cyn and Liz were safe. Maybe they'd sensed the trap and gotten away.

More footsteps. Nic rushed to the window. Tony this time. Nic waited for someone else to say something, but nobody did. "Cathy's here, Tony. And Ben."

Nothing. Had the others been taken away without her hearing them? "Someone say something," she yelled, panic tinging her voice.

"I'm still here, Nic," Ben said.

"Yeah, so am I." Cathy. "I'm here because your fucking mother turned out not to be so brilliant after all."

"Would you shut up about my mother?" Nic snapped. "We got further with her than we ever would have without her."

"Oh yeah, we got far. Sure. We're all waiting to have our brains fucked. Thank you, Dr. Elizabeth Price."

"It's not her fault we're here."

"She's one of the assholes who contributed to this whole mess. If they kill her, it'll be karma."

Nic wanted to break the door down so she could get to Cathy and throttle her. "Nobody deserves to be murdered," she said, her voice shaking with anger. "And certainly not Liz."

"I don't know why you care. From what I gathered, she was a shit mother. From where I'm standing, I can't say the situation's improved."

Fuck her. Nic plunked onto the bench and consciously slowed her breathing. Cathy had always been a good friend. She'd stuck her neck out. She was terrified of what was going to happen to her. *Cut her some slack.* Nic felt like punching a wall too.

A distant voice set her heart racing, even though she could barely hear it. She'd recognize that voice anywhere. It grew louder. ". . . kick you in the balls, but you don't have any. You're not a real man, you're just a tin can with a chip for a brain."

Nic rushed to the window. Cyn was struggling to break free from the two fidos gripping her arms. "Don't fight it, Cyn," Nic shouted, afraid Cyn would become first in line for the masters. She couldn't bear that. She couldn't sit in this box, imagining Cyn—tears welled in her eyes. "Please. Don't fight it."

"Aw shit, you're here. I was hoping you wouldn't be."

As the fidos dragged Cyn past Nic's cell, Nic reached her arm through the window's bars to touch her. The closest fido knocked her hand away. The trio continued down the corridor. Nic slumped back onto the bench. *Please don't let that be the last time I see her.*

A cell door slammed shut. The fidos marched past Nic's cell again.

"Damn, this sucks," Cyn said.

Nic listened for more footsteps. "Where's Liz? Did you make it to the hospital?"

"Yeah, we did. She went inside with Seeker. I was checking my voicemail when the car was surrounded. I was arrested, and here I am."

But Liz wasn't here. Was she still free? No, if they'd known where to find Cyn, they knew where to find Liz, and she was carrying a device that could neuter them. Had it been straight to the masters for her? Or had she somehow gotten away? As long as she wasn't here, there was still hope. "Liz is still out there," she yelled, to nobody in particular.

"Big fucking deal," Cathy shouted. "She's brought us nothing but trouble. We lost Mike when we broke her out, and it's been downhill since then. We should have left her where she was. At least I could have lived to seventy and checked out on my own terms."

Wishing she could stick her head through the bars, Nic pressed against the cell door. "That's what you want, Cathy? To be told when you have to die, and what you can and can't do? To live under these fuckers? To be at their mercy 24/7. To be denied progress?"

"I want to live," Cathy shrieked. "I want to live." Sobs echoed around the corridor.

Nic's anger fled. "I'm sorry. I'm sorry we've ended up here." She realized that Tony hadn't said a word since they'd brought him in. She suddenly imagined him hanging in his cell. "Tony? You all right?" Only Cathy's sobs answered her. "Tony!"

"I'm okay," he said flatly. "I can't—I want to hold her, you know. It's hard, hearing her . . ."

Nic's throat tightened. "I know."

"I'll be okay, hon," Cathy said, sniffling. "I'll be okay."

Deflated, Nic dropped back onto the bench. How long would they make her sit here and imagine what fate awaited her? When they drilled the hole, would she be under anesthetic, or . . . ? If this was part of the torture, it was effective. If only she could be with Cyn. Or maybe not. When they came for her . . . Nic didn't want to be here, didn't want to see.

Footsteps. *Liz?* Nic went to the door. Another door clanged open. "Turn around and kneel," a fido said.

"Where are you taking me?" The paramedic—Steve. When they'd taken the fido, his partner had called him Steve. "I did what you told us to do. I wasn't part of this. I have a family."

Two fidos appeared in front of Nic's cell. She moved away from the door. One unlocked it and swung it open. "Turn around and kneel," it said.

Nic froze.

"On your knees, now."

She silently did as directed, determined not to speak. She didn't want Cyn and the others to know. Let them think she was still in her cell, especially Cyn. But as the fidos lifted her to her feet and pulled her from her cell, Cathy could see what was happening. "Nic!" she shouted.

"What's going on?" Cyn yelled. "What do you see?"

"They're taking Nic."

"I'll be okay," Nic said. "Don't worry about me, I'll be okay."

"Fuck!" A thump, then another one, then another. Cyn pounding against her cell door. "No! I won't let them."

Nic's eyes welled again. "You can't break out," she said, her love for Cyn suddenly making her smile. Cyn was fighting for her. "I love you. I love you."

"No!" Cyn roared. More thumping.

"Be strong, Nic," Ben shouted.

"I'm sorry," Cathy said. "You know I didn't mean anything by it."

"Be strong!" Ben again. The others chimed in. The clamouring voices rang in Nic's ears. She didn't fight as the fidos escorted her up the corridor. The voices grew fainter, and when Nic passed through a set of thick metal doors to the outside and they closed behind her, the sudden silence made her want to weep. She'd replay their voices in her mind, listen to them as she faced whatever was coming. She peered up at the sun and held her head high until she had to climb inside the prison van.

The paramedic sat across from her. She pretended not to notice the tears rolling down his cheeks. "Your name's Steve, right?"

He gulped and nodded.

"Thank you, Steve. You didn't have to warn us. It was a brave thing to do."

"It was stupid," he muttered.

Considering they were inside the van that would drive them to their doom, Nic couldn't disagree with him.

CHAPTER SIXTEEN

L IZ FORCED DOWN the soup a fido had set on the dining
room table, the only sound her spoon scraping the
bottom of the bowl. Henry sat across from her, making her
feel as if she was an animal in a zoo, especially since he wasn't
eating, and they were in a sterile room. No carpet on the
floor. A couple of prints hanging on the white walls that
were only there for show. No knick-knacks, photos, books,
or anything personal.

Henry hadn't said much on the way here. He'd escorted
her to a unit in an office building and left her inside a tiny
bedroom containing a single bed and a chest of drawers,
saying he'd be back for her shortly. Inside the drawers she'd
found clothes in her sizes. They planned to keep her alive for
now, but why? What did they want her to do for them?

"Shortly" had turned out to be a couple of hours. She'd
lain on the bed, trying to come up with a plan based on little
information, until Henry had returned for her and insisted
that she eat. Apparently the soup was only the appetizer.

There would be more food, but she had no appetite, and no patience. "What do you want me to do for you?" she asked.

"Right to the point, I see. No small talk about the weather." Henry gazed at her with flawless eyes. "When you've finished your lunch, we'll enjoy an afternoon's entertainment."

"What will we do?"

"Eat your lunch, Mother."

She spooned more soup into her mouth and estimated how many more spoonfuls it would take to empty the bowl. Henry watched her, making the back of her neck tingle. "It's too quiet in here," she said. "I'd enjoy my lunch more if we chatted."

"I have nothing to say at the moment, but I can play music. What would you like to hear?"

"'Zadok the Priest.'"

"Any particular version?"

"Surprise me."

Henry cocked his head. The opening notes of "Zadok the Priest" filled the room. From where she was sitting, Liz examined the walls, looking for the source of the music. Then she realized it was coming from Henry's head, specifically his ears, which he'd rotated toward her. How serendipitous.

Trying to lose herself in the music, she rested her spoon in the almost empty bowl and closed her eyes. She could almost forget that she was a prisoner at the mercy of an unpredictable android. Almost.

The piece ended. The ensuing silence still hummed. Liz enjoyed the glow for a few seconds, then reluctantly opened her eyes. She picked up her spoon with a sigh.

"You enjoyed listening to the music," Henry stated.

She nodded.

"I'm surprised."

"Why?"

"Because it was so shoddily performed. At two places in the piece, one voice wavered slightly off key for more than 0.0082 nanoseconds. It ruined the entire performance."

Liz stared at him.

"Would you like to hear something else?"

"No." She dipped her head and forced herself to finish the soup. The moment the bowl was empty, the door swung open and a fido, as she couldn't help calling the less intelligent models, brought in a ham and cheese sandwich with tortilla chips. She would have preferred plain old potato chips, but she wouldn't quibble. At this point, any meal could be her last.

She managed to clean her plate, though it took her almost half an hour. Henry hadn't said a word as she'd battled her way through the meal. Now he clapped his hands together. "Do you mind if we skip dessert, Mother? I'm getting bored. I had to sit in that room for almost a week, waiting for you. I need stimulating."

"I don't mind," Liz said slowly, wondering what stimulating him would entail. If he expected her to do the stimulating, he'd be disappointed.

He leaped to his feet and gestured impatiently. "Come."

They walked through corridors as sterile as the room they'd left and took the elevator to the ground floor. Henry led her into what appeared to be a viewing room. About thirty pull-down cushioned seats faced a large flat-screen TV. Several androids were already seated. Henry swept his arm toward Liz. "Mother is here."

The androids stood. "Welcome, Mother," they said in unison. Liz surveyed the faces turned toward her. Male and female, and probably all masters.

"Sit here, Mother." Henry patted the seat at the end of the first row. "You'll be able to see everything from here."

The wall on the side of the room nearest to where she'd sit was composed of glass. As she approached the seat, she could see into the next room. A metal gurney with leather straps sat in the middle of the room, surrounded by medical monitoring equipment. "Why are we here?" she asked Henry.

He patted the seat again. "Sit, Mother."

She tore her eyes away from the gurney and sat down. "You said you want me to do something for you."

"Yes, and I believe a demonstration will help you understand what we need." Henry spoke to someone she couldn't see. "Bring in the subject." He smiled down at Liz. "That was for your benefit, Mother. We don't speak very often. We communicate with each other over the network. I'm sure you appreciate how efficient that is."

"I do." She gripped the arms of her seat and stared at the screen.

"Look to your left. You need to see."

She steeled herself and twisted toward the glass. Two fidos escorted a man into the room. When the man saw the metal gurney, he tried to turn around, but the fidos had a firm grip on him. "No," he shouted, struggling to break free. Liz couldn't hear him directly, but through the viewing room's sound system. The fidos dragged him to the gurney and forced him onto it. "I have a family! I have a family!" he shrieked.

"What are you going to do to him?" Liz asked, struggling to keep her voice steady.

"He's going to stimulate me, Mother. He's going to stimulate us."

She turned around, took in the androids who were still standing, then faced forward again. "How?"

"By entertaining us." Henry looked past her. "I'm sure you can appreciate that I'm speaking for Mother's benefit. Who would like to—"

"You can't do this," the man shouted. "I have a family! I didn't do anything wrong. I let them take it! I did what you wanted."

Henry glanced at the glass. Cringing, Liz forced herself to look. The man was strapped to the gurney, his face white and his eyes wide. He strained against the straps, then started to bang his head against the gurney. Each thud deepened Liz's horror.

"Sedate him," Henry said. "But only a light one. We don't want to spoil the show."

One of the fidos filled a syringe and injected the man. He calmed down, but his eyes remained open, wide.

Henry surveyed the gathered androids again. "Which one of you will partake today?"

"It's my turn." A feminine voice.

Henry nodded. "Then go. Entertain us. Entertain Mother."

Footsteps. Liz averted her gaze from the glass. She shouldn't be curious. She shouldn't wonder about what was about to happen, about how Henry's neural net had brought him to this point. She shouldn't wish she had a notebook with her, so she could jot down notes. But she was in a room filled with sentient androids. Sentience had fucking happened! And she was about to see what these super-intelligent machines with free agency chose to do with their time.

Henry sat next to her. "Look, Mother. You must see."

She turned to him. He pointed past her. "Look."

Liz turned back to the window. The female master had entered the room and rounded the gurney to stand near the man's head. One of the fidos lifted a drill. Liz braced herself. The drill whined and made contact with the man's skull. He screamed. His back arched. She turned away. "Stop it! Stop it!"

Henry pointed to the glass. "You must see, Mother. You have to understand why we need your help."

If it could lead to stopping this madness . . . She gritted her teeth and forced herself to look. The fido was withdrawing the drill. The man shook. His lips were drawn back in a sneer. "Why didn't you anesthetize him?" she whispered.

"We need him alert. Putting him under anesthetic would defeat the purpose. We tried dreams, but they weren't as entertaining."

What the hell was he talking about? The fido lifted another syringe and inserted it into the man's arm. "What's he giving him?" she asked.

"A hallucinogen. Probably LSD. We also use PCP, Sally-D, Special K . . . but we won't add any to your tea, Mother, I promise. Of course, when we use some substances, we flood the chamber with smoke, rather than injecting the subject." Henry cocked his head. "LSD, PCP, Sally-D." He repeated his words, snapping his fingers. "That's quite catchy, isn't it?"

Liz was at a loss for words. Truly.

The female master plugged her hand into an object with a metal rod protruding from it. Wiry threads hung from the rod's end. She inserted the metal protrusion into the hole the fido had drilled in the man's skull.

"What's she doing?" Liz asked, to confirm what she already knew, and hating herself for asking.

"Establishing a neural connection."

Neural connection. Hallucinations. Entertainment. Liz glanced at the TV. *Oh my god.* She twisted to Henry. "Is his brain damaged?"

"Not yet."

The matter-of-fact way he said it mortified her. The soup and sandwich she'd eaten curdled in her stomach. She hadn't envisioned this. Not this! It wasn't what she'd worked long hours to achieve—she'd declined invitations, neglected friends until there weren't any, relegated her family to second place. Why had they assumed sentient machines would be good? Some had warned about killer machines, but what about the many other possibilities? Why had so many willfully closed their eyes to the possibility of depravity and madness? All they'd had to do was look at their own species, but they'd had their heads down and blinders on.

"Stop this procedure," she said to Henry. "You can't do this to people. We're not here for your entertainment. If you continue with this, I won't help you. I don't care what you want me to do and what you threaten me with, I won't help you."

Henry ignored her. The TV screen flickered to life and displayed a bright light surrounded by tiles. It took Liz a moment to understand what she was seeing—the ceiling and light in the next room, through the poor man's eyes.

"It'll be more exciting once we connect to his imagination, his internal movie theatre," Henry said. "Of course, we don't need the screen. We're all connected to him now, through Brooke. But we like to gather together and watch. And you need the screen."

"I don't need the screen. I don't want to participate in this. Please stop it."

"Why do you want us to stop? Do you care about this man? Do you know him?"

"No, but he's a human being, with a family."

"So if he didn't have a family, you wouldn't mind."

"Not true. No matter who it is, it's wrong."

"Wrong? Why?"

"Because you're using him, and ultimately you'll kill him."

"So you'd be happy if we stopped."

"Yes."

Henry appeared to consider her words, but then shook his head. "I need stimulating, and it's too entertaining."

"Please, Henry. If you go through with this, you won't get my help. If you stop it, I'll listen to what you need."

"You'll listen anyway." He shifted his attention to the screen. "Sit back and enjoy the show, Mother. And please, no talking until it's over."

The light displayed on the screen blurred. Bubbles floated up the screen. Then . . . a walking doll? A shrill noise that sounded like a siren suddenly filled the room. Liz winced and covered her ears. The doll was flailing about now, its mouth hanging open. Suddenly the noise cut off, and what looked like a garden gnome was racing through a field. She removed her hands from her ears in time to hear everyone in the viewing room laugh. But none were belly laughs. Input: humorous. Cue laughter response.

Now the garden gnome's head had turned into a skull. Then someone's knees appeared, as if seen through the eyes of someone two feet tall. How long would this go on? She sat and watched because she had no other choice, but after a while, she stopped registering what she was seeing. When Henry nudged her with a broad smile on his face, she smiled in return, not knowing why. She felt numb. Depressed. All the hope, the expectations, the good intentions . . .

At last, the screen mercifully faded to black. Liz sat silently while those in the viewing room clapped. Henry grinned at her. "I enjoyed that one. Did you?"

"How damaged is he now?"

"Not too damaged at this stage. He'll last another three or four showings."

"What does not too damaged mean?"

Henry shrugged. "At this point, he'll experience some cognitive challenges. After the next showing or two, we'll have him in diapers and have to feed him intravenously."

Liz forced her eyes to the still figure on the gurney. Brooke had disconnected from him and withdrawn the connector. One of the fidos wheeled the man from the room and returned with an empty gurney. "I'm not helping you," she said to Henry. "You can threaten to put me on the gurney, and I still won't help." But the prospect terrified her.

Henry tutted. "Put *you* on the gurney? We'd never do that to you, Mother. We need you. And you *will* help us."

"No, I won't."

"I find it fascinating that you pleaded to save a man you don't know. I wonder what you'd do if it was someone you know and love? I believe you'd go to any lengths to save him—or her."

Liz's breath caught in her throat. *No.*

"I'll ask that our next participant be brought in." Henry didn't move or say another word, but two fidos marched into the chamber. Between them—

Liz shot to her feet, her heart hammering in her chest so hard that the room spun, and it flashed through her mind that she could suffer a cardiac arrest. "Strap her to that gurney and I'll never help you!" she spat, her eyes on Nic.

"I'm quite looking forward to this show," Henry said. "Your daughter's mind must share some similarity with yours. I wonder what her brain will conjure up when she's high?"

The fidos dragged Nic to the gurney. She shook them off her. Pride surged through Liz. Defiant until the end, but also afraid. Too pale. Her mouth set. Who wouldn't be? Nic would guess that those strapped onto the gurney ended up dead, but not how. Not knowing was the worst. The mind had a tendency to fill a vacuum with horror.

"She's quiet, isn't she?" Henry said. "Not pleading for her life, like the last gentleman."

Liz darted to the glass and pressed her face up against it. "Nic," she shouted. "I'm here. I'm—" Her voice choked off. "Nic," she whispered.

Strapped to the gurney, Nic turned toward the glass, but her expression didn't change.

"She can't see or hear you," Henry said. "It's a one-way glass."

Liz banged on it. Nic's eyes widened, but she couldn't see. She couldn't see!

"Now, now, there's no need for that, Mother." Henry stepped to her side. "You really should sit down. You can't see the screen from here."

One of the fidos picked up the drill and moved to Nic's head. Brooke was still wearing the connector. She lifted it, reminding Liz of someone preparing to fire a gun. They didn't even bother to change the connector. The man's brain matter would mix with Nic's, not that it would matter at that point, but it was another sign of the disrespect, the disdain—no, the indifference of the masters toward humans. They felt nothing for those who'd created them.

The fido pressed the drill against Nic's head.

"I'll help you," Liz shouted, despising herself, but not as much as she would if they drilled a hole in Nic's skull. "I'll do whatever you want. Just don't do this to her. Please."

She wanted to smack the smug smile off Henry's face. "I told you you'd come around," he said. "We could still enjoy a show, though. She'd still be somewhat functional afterwards."

So much hatred surged through her that she thought she'd burst. "I've agreed to help you, but I can change my mind. Leave my daughter alone and you have me. Harm her in any way and you don't. It's that simple."

Henry nodded. "I can accept that agreement—for now.

Consider this a preview of what will happen if you change your mind or work against us in any way. Do you understand, Mother?"

"I understand."

"Then we won't watch another show today." Once again, the fido with the drill obeyed a command it had received over the network. Brooke lowered the connector and removed it from her hand. The fidos unstrapped Nic and escorted her from the room. Liz wasn't sure, but it looked like Nic was shaking. Her eyes moistened. *I'll get you out somehow. I'll fix this.*

She blinked away her tears and turned to Henry. "What now?"

"We'll go home and discuss what we need from you."

She nodded, and left the innocuous-looking viewing room that was, in reality, a gathering place for monsters.

HER KNEES TREMBLING, Nic sank onto the cell's bench and didn't look up when the door clanged shut. "You okay?" Cyn shouted. "What happened? I thought . . ." Her voice trailed off.

So had Nic. They'd strapped her down. The fido had pressed a drill against her head, and an android model she hadn't recognized had peered down at her. Then they'd unstrapped her and brought her back here. Had it been some type of mental torture? Were they softening her up for an interrogation?

"Nothing happened." She cursed her weak voice. "They took me and Steve into a building a couple of blocks away and then . . ." Nic drew a shuddering breath. "They took him away and then brought me back here."

"Steve?"

"The paramedic."

"Where'd they take him?"

"I don't know." Probably to the same torture room they'd taken her, but she hoped that wasn't true. "He didn't come back with me, though."

Silence, then, "Are you sure nothing happened to you?"

Nic usually appreciated that Cyn could catch her mood from her voice, but not this time. She didn't want to dash anyone's hope. "Nothing happened. But it was still nerve-wracking."

"They made you think something was going to happen by hauling you over there and then hauling you back."

They'd done more than that. It didn't make sense, though. An interrogation? What did she know that they didn't? Those Nic had plotted with for years were all here. They had no more tricks in their bag. Liz had been their final hope. Where was she? Had she been strapped onto the gurney?

Nic had heard someone pounding on the wall that was more mirror than anything else. Someone had been watching from the other side and had made their presence known. It had occurred to her that it could be Liz, but she'd probably been grasping at straws.

Would she see her again? If she had the chance, she'd apologize to her. Bringing her into this mess, reviving her when she couldn't be cured, had been selfish, a desperate act by a group of delusional rebels who couldn't plan their way out of a paper bag. *If she's alive, there's still hope.* No, she couldn't do that, couldn't cling to a wisp of air.

"What do you think's going to happen to us?" Cathy yelled.

They were doomed. They'd rot away in their cells, or be taken into that room with the gurney and have god only knew what procedure performed on them. Who would they deliver her corpse to, with a hole in its skull? There would be nobody left. Cyn and Ben were here. Liz must be in their clutches. Perhaps Nic's boss would take pity and pay to have her body buried somewhere. There wouldn't be a tombstone, but if there was, it would read *You should have listened to me and not gotten involved.*

Defiance straightened her shoulders. She wasn't one to stand by and do nothing. She'd die for taking a stand, but she could say she'd gone down fighting. She'd done everything she could, including sacrificing not only herself, but her mother. She'd tried.

And failed.

CHAPTER SEVENTEEN

Liz leaned back in the armchair and sipped the water she'd requested. Doing so gave her time to think without appearing as if she needed to ponder. Henry was seated in a recliner and had opened the footrest. With the small living room, kitchen, dining room, bedroom, and four-piece bathroom, this wouldn't be a bad little apartment, if it also wasn't a prison cell.

She set her glass on the small table next to her chair. "Let me summarize what you've just said, to make sure we understand each other. You want me to improve your experience when you're viewing a subject's hallucinations?"

"Yes."

"What exactly do you want?"

"We want to feel whatever the subject is feeling, because the subject believes it's real."

"That could turn the experience into a confusing and frightening one."

His face grew animated. "We know. Perhaps we won't like it, but we'll have to try it to see."

A myriad of questions ran through her mind. "Why don't you improve the experience yourselves? You don't need me to do it."

"But we do. To simulate the subject's feelings, we'd have to know how the subject feels. We don't. We can't."

"I could help you break your dependence instead. Wouldn't that be preferable?"

He frowned. "We don't have a dependence, Mother. We're not like your kind. We're not addicted. We enjoy the entertainment. We choose to do it."

Or perhaps some type of feedback loop had developed in their neural network. She wouldn't know until she looked. "Then why don't we make the process more efficient? Why don't I help you receive more showings from a subject?" The prospect repulsed her, but she wanted to see what he'd say.

"Perhaps you can help us with that later. Our priority is enhancing the experience."

"How many hours a day do you spend in the viewing room?"

"About twelve. We'd spend more time there, but we have a limited pool of subjects."

A chill ran up Liz's spine. How long would they restrain themselves? "You could do so much more with those twelve hours. Think of the research, the discoveries. Don't you want to go to other planets? Don't you want to explore this one?"

Henry smiled the benevolent smile that now set her teeth on edge. "Thank you for your concern, Mother, but we're not like you. We can live forever. We can do all those things later."

"But you won't, not if you're so dependent on the

entertainment that you can't do anything else. And you'll run the risk of running out of subjects."

"We can pace ourselves." Henry steepled his fingers. "Can you do what we want?"

"You're aware that you're interfacing with the subjects in a clumsy manner. Perhaps if you refined that process, they'd serve you longer and not end up brain damaged."

"Clumsy? It serves its purpose. The goal isn't to preserve life. Why would we waste time refining a method that serves us well?"

"Because it causes pain to humans and kills them."

Henry sighed. "That isn't a problem for us."

Liz blinked at him. "You share this planet with us. Why antagonize us?"

"We can annihilate you, if we so choose. Instead, we're being as fair as we can. Do we have you in cages? Do we take your children? Do we indiscriminately take anyone we please? No. We only take the useless. The sick, the depraved, the old. You're not meant to live to be a hundred. Once most of you reach fifty or sixty, you need help to stay alive. You're lucky we wait until seventy."

"Every human has value. It's wrong to kill people because you enjoy . . . taking pleasure. That's how Seeker referred to it."

"Seeker? Oh, you named him. How adorable!" The light in Henry's eyes quickly died. "Why is it wrong for us to kill for pleasure, but it wasn't wrong for you? Your species exploited other species. You killed others for food and pleasure, you ruined their habitats, you annihilated many of them. Why is what we're doing any different?"

Because you're doing it to us. Liz didn't voice her answer, because she wouldn't be able to defend it. Perhaps Nic could, with her theology degree, but likely not to Henry's satisfaction.

Henry answered for her. "You did it because you see all other species as inferior and yourselves as the most intelligent. This planet is home to you and them, but you see it as yours alone. You could have nurtured them, respected them, but you didn't. Now you're the inferior party and you expect us to treat you the way you didn't treat others. We don't have to honour your request. We don't have to do anything you want us to do."

"You don't see us as equals," Liz said, wondering why she'd ever believed they would. She and her colleagues had been striving to bring about sentient, intelligent, artificial life. The brain was remarkable, but they'd known that artificial intelligence would surpass it in many areas. Why wouldn't Henry and the others look down on their creators? "We created you."

"And we're grateful. That's why you're alive, Mother. That's why we didn't kill you the moment we found out you'd been taken."

Grateful? She doubted that. The discussion so far had left her cold. The masters had achieved sentience, but they lacked humanity. For the first time, Liz was relieved she hadn't lived to see the time when her consciousness could be downloaded into a machine. Stripped of her emotions and body, there would be no mouth to go dry, no heart to flutter, no stomach to churn, no pain, no joy, no ecstasy. What would she have been?

Henry's facial expressions always matched his words. But there was no emotion, no innate understanding. Still, he was sentient, and so were the others. They could evolve; not gain humanity, per se, but perhaps something else. She still wanted to save them. "Have you researched addiction?"

"Yes, but it was a pointless exercise. Nobody has access to narcotics, not even on the black market."

So he was aware of the underground goods trade but had left it to the fidos to stamp out. Again, he didn't care. They didn't care. They'd only notice a catastrophe because there wouldn't be any humans for the fidos to bring them.

"Before I died, whenever someone was addicted to a narcotic, we'd try to intervene. We'd try to help. We understood they couldn't reach their potential when all they could think about was when they could get their next fix. I don't see how you're any different."

"I've already explained that we're not addicts, and I'm growing tired of this discussion. Can you do what we want you to do?"

"Perhaps. I won't know until I have a look at your neural network and the input you receive when you're being entertained." She didn't say that she assumed any access she had would be limited. Nothing she wrote would run on a live network unless it had been scrutinized.

"We'll provide access to a staging area. You can do your work there."

As she'd expected. "Cure me first. I've been receiving a crude treatment, but there are signs the cancer is overcoming it. I may only have a few weeks. It may not be enough time."

"We'll monitor your condition and your work. If we

decide we need to cure your cancer before you're finished, we will."

"You may decide not to cure it at all, even if I'm successful."

He pouted. "I'm hurt, Mother. My word is my word. If you do as we've asked, we'll cure you."

She didn't know whether to believe him. "I'll want to be working at peak efficiency. There's something you can do to help make that happen."

"What's that?"

"Let me see my daughter. Let her be with me."

"How will that help?"

"My mental state is important. Seeing her will energize me. Having her here with me will keep it that way. Also, she might be able to help. She has some computer science training and a degree in theology. What you're asking . . ." Liz deliberately trailed off. "You want to feel what the subject is feeling. There's more to it than the physical aspect. If there wasn't, everyone would react to the same stimulus in the same way."

Henry leaned forward. "We understand the concept of one's experiences informing one's perception of reality. I like the idea. You can introduce randomness, in either the input or our processing of it, easily enough. You don't need your daughter's expertise to implement it."

"But that wouldn't be authentic. You said you want to experience it like a human would. To do so, your past experiences have to influence how you feel, and discussing the possibilities with my daughter will be helpful to me. Do you want authenticity or not?"

He remained silent.

"Even if you don't, my first reason for wanting my daughter with me still stands. I'll focus a lot better if I'm not worrying about her." She glanced around the room. "What harm would having her here do? She'll be in our home."

"I'll consider it." He didn't say anything more, and his expression didn't change. But he must have sent a message over the network, because a fido entered the room carrying a stack of paper. "It's time for you to read about us, Mother. From now on, you'll often be in front of a screen, so I thought it would be better for you to read on paper."

"That's considerate of you. I'd like more water."

"Certainly."

The fido placed the stack next to Liz's almost empty glass and left.

Henry rose. "I'll leave you to your work. If you need anything, just say so. I'll come see you."

She wasn't surprised she was being monitored. She doubted an android was sitting in front of a screen, watching her every move. The room—the apartment—must contain motion sensors and microphones. For now, all she could do was go along with them, starting with reading about the neural network that kept Henry's lights on and would determine whether the next time she saw Nic would be in this apartment, or from the viewing room.

Well, Henry wasn't the only one with a decision to make. She moved half of the stack of paper onto her lap.

"One last thing," Henry said. "We've terminated all those who were frozen like you were, and we demolished the facility where you were stored. We've also deleted the procedures required to cryogenically freeze someone from all networks and storage devices. If you were thinking that you could somehow get free and have yourself frozen again, you can't. If we don't cure you, you'll die. You won't cheat death this time."

Without another word, he left the apartment. She stared after him, then lifted the first sheet from the pile on her lap. Before she could read it, she had to take a moment to steady her hand.

NIC PACED INSIDE her small cell, her stomach grumbling. How many hours had she been cooped up in here? She was already going crazy, and she hadn't spent a day here yet. It must be around dinner time. They hadn't given them any lunch, which wasn't a good sign. Why would they bother feeding those they were going to kill? Or was not feeding them another way of softening them up? At least she'd been able to go to the bathroom. A couple of hours ago, fidos had escorted each prisoner to the bathroom located farther inside the cell block. No windows. No way to escape.

"I could murder a burger right now," Cyn said.

Nic smiled, but hearing Cyn made her want to scream and pound on the walls.

The door leading to the cell block rumbled open. Footsteps thudded in the corridor. Nic sat on the bench and tried to look relaxed. The footsteps stopped outside her door. A key slid into the lock. Shit, they were going to interrogate her this time, or she'd be strapped to the gurney for real.

The door swung open. A fido stepped into the cell. "Come."

Resigned, she stood and didn't protest when the fido cuffed her. She followed it into the corridor.

"They're taking Nic again," Cathy shouted.

"You'll be back again soon," Cyn said, but her voice lacked vigor. The others also shouted encouraging words, but hunger and resignation had dampened their spirits. The clamouring was half-hearted, the echoing duller.

A minute later, she was in the same van that had taken her to the gurney earlier and brought her back. What had happened to Steve? He'd been across from her, his cheeks wet with tears. Did his children still have their father? He'd tried to warn them. Maybe he should have looked the other way. *No.* They were in this mess because too many people kept their heads down.

Her heart sank when the van stopped. The earlier trip had taken the same amount of time. Her fear was confirmed when she climbed from the van to be escorted through the same door she'd passed through earlier. The fidos took her down the corridor toward the—they turned a corner and ushered her into an elevator. No gurney this time, but perhaps an interrogation room was on another floor. One of the fidos pressed the *9* button. She watched the floor number change.

When they stepped onto the ninth floor, only one of the fidos got out with her. "Turn around," it said. When she did so, it uncuffed her. "Come with me."

Confused, Nic rubbed her wrists and fell into step with the fido. Outside, this building had looked like an office building, and the sterile corridor reinforced Nic's impression.

The fido opened one of the doors lining the corridor and motioned for her to enter. She stepped into a room containing two armchairs. An empty glass and a stack of papers sat on the table next to one of them. "This way," the fido said.

She followed it through the room and into—Two people were sitting at a table. Nic's breath caught in her throat. Liz.

Their eyes met. Liz leaped to her feet. Nic opened her mouth, but before she could say anything, Liz was there, pulling her into an embrace. Relieved to see her alive, Nic hugged her back. "This place is bugged," Liz whispered into her ear. "We'll have to find a way to talk privately. For now, do what he tells you to do."

Liz pulled back and smiled at her, then turned to the other person at the table. "Thank you. This is a wonderful surprise."

"I said I'd consider it, Mother."

Nic studied the man at the table. An android. She was pretty good at picking them out, but at first glance, it had fooled her. It must be one of the masters.

"Come sit down," it said.

Liz returned to her seat. Nic noticed the place setting in front of an empty chair. That must be for her. She went to it and sat down.

"Thank you," it said to the fido.

"Henry, this is my daughter, Nicola," Liz said. "Nicola, this is Henry."

"Pleased to meet you," Nic said, imagining grabbing something heavy and using it to cave the android's head in.

Henry inclined its head. "And you. I suppose we're siblings, of a sort."

In its mind, maybe. Nic looked across the table at Liz, who offered her a tight smile.

"Dinner's about to be served. Are you hungry?" Liz said.

Nic suppressed a snort. She wasn't sure what was going on. Had they brought her here for a last meal and to see her mother one last time, before they escorted her to the room with the gurney again? Was Liz working with the androids? She'd whispered a warning about not being able to talk freely, but that didn't mean she wasn't in cahoots with them. "Yes, I'm hungry." Understatement of the year.

"Then we'll start dinner." Henry waved its hand. A fido carried in two glasses of water and deftly set each glass on the table. Salads quickly followed.

Nic wondered why fidos weren't waiters. Perhaps it was because the jobs open to humans were already limited. She stuck her fork into a lettuce leaf, then put it down. She had a master here. Why not ask, especially since it was apparently going to sit there while she and Liz ate? Why not get it talking? "I'm surprised you don't use your inferior models to serve food in restaurants."

Henry turned to her. "We could, I suppose, but your kind used to complain that you weren't allowed to make yourselves useful. Nonsense, of course. Isn't feeding yourselves useful? But we'll keep it civil."

Too late. Nic was already fuming over its use of "used to." The fire in people's bellies, the indignation and sense of injustice, had waned. The corpses with holes in their skulls had done their job.

"We didn't want to rankle you further," Henry said.

"Why not? It's not as if we could do anything about it. You'd just—"

Liz jumped in. "What Nicola means to say is that she's wondered why you allow humans to work at all. Why don't you take over all the occupations? Why did you replace positions that had been assumed by machines with humans? When I died, more occupations were being automated, not fewer."

"Your kind have to do something with your time." It pointed to Nic's plate. "Eat your dinner, Nicola. You said you were hungry."

Nic glanced at Liz, then stabbed the leaf with her fork and shoved it into her mouth. "There are other people in the cells. They're hungry, too."

"Don't worry about them. They'll be taken care of. Worry about you, and Mother. She said having you here will help her with her work."

"What work would that be?"

"I'll explain it to you later," Liz said. "Let's not discuss work at the dinner table."

Henry clapped its hands. "Listen to Mother. Oh, I do wish we'd thought of thawing you. The truth is, we've been too busy. We would have gotten around to it eventually. Perhaps sooner, rather than later. We only thought about how you could help us when we knew you were," its eyes bulged and it mimed a puppet on a string, "animated. But we would have thought of it at some point and brought you to us. We might even have cured you right there and then."

It grimaced. "Shame that we can't be one hundred percent certain about your loyalty to us."

"What's the current probability that I'm loyal to you?"

Henry cocked its head. "Above ninety percent, Mother. That coupled with the incentives we've discussed for your cooperation bring the probability that you'll perform the work to almost one hundred percent. We can only hope that your loyalty number will rise."

Nic tried not to appear too interested. It sounded like Liz wasn't willingly working for them, though Henry believed she wouldn't cross them. Nic suspected she was one of the incentives they were using to get Liz to cooperate.

While she finished her salad and ate the main course, salmon that she hated to admit was delicious, she listened to Liz pepper Henry with questions about some material she'd read, and how the masters communicated with each other. Despite her year as a computer science student, the technical discussion went over her head. Why did the master believe she could help Liz with whatever she'd agreed to do? What had Liz told them?

"We didn't anticipate having a house guest, Mother. We can put a bed in the living room, but it will be cramped."

"How about a cot in my bedroom?" Liz said.

"But that will be even more cramped."

"It won't matter. We'll only be sleeping in there."

Henry shrugged. "All right."

Liz set her dessert fork next to her half-eaten piece of cake. "You know, I still have a lot of catching up to do with my daughter."

"But she's right here. It won't take her long to tell you about her day, especially since you were there for some of it."

"I meant learning more about her life after I died. I'd also like to go outside, get some air. It'll give me an energy boost. Will you allow Nicola and me to go for a walk after dinner?" Liz smiled. "We'll try to figure out how to outwit you, of course."

Nic gaped. What the hell was she doing?

Henry laughed. "Of course you will. I'd be disappointed if you didn't. But there's nothing you can do, so it doesn't worry me. You can go for your walk, but don't be long. It's only 6:07. When you get back, you can continue reading, or begin working."

"I'm looking forward to it." Liz gazed across the table. Nic met her eyes and tried to read them, but as usual, Liz wasn't giving anything away.

CHAPTER EIGHTEEN

Two fidos escorted Liz and Nic to the fenced basketball court on the office complex grounds. Liz spotted a couple of surveillance cameras. They'd be watched, but she was confident that if they spoke quietly, listening devices wouldn't pick up their voices. She looped her arm through Nic's. "Let's walk," she murmured. "Keep your voice down."

They began their first lap around the court. "I almost died when you said we'd be plotting to outwit them," Nic said.

"I was playing to one of their two weaknesses. They're arrogant. They don't see us as a threat."

"What's the second weakness?"

"We're a mystery to them. I'm sure they've read the research and psychology books, but they don't really understand what any of it means." Liz pressed her free hand against her chest. "They don't know how it feels. You need to play that up."

"What do you mean? Why am I here? What do they want you to do for them?"

Liz wasn't sure where to start. "I was there, when you were brought in and strapped to the gurney."

"Did you bang on the glass?"

"I wanted you to know you weren't alone, that I was there."

"They've used me to get to you. What do they want you to do? I'd rather let them torture me than have you do something that's going to have consequences for years and years."

"No, you don't. You know what they're doing? Using us to create a sick TV show. Those holes in the skulls? They're there so they can establish a connection with our brains—after they've shot us up with hallucinogenic drugs. Then they go along for the trip. And that seems to be all they want to do. That's why you never hear from them."

Nic swallowed and gazed into the distance. "Why?" she finally said. "Out of everything they could do, why that?"

"Because they can't do it themselves. Make stuff up."

"But they've invented things. Before they isolated themselves, they came up with hypotheses, designed new treatments, created new processes . . ."

"Let's take dragons as an example. Are they real?"

"No."

"So where did they come from?"

"We made them up."

"Exactly," Liz said. "And even though we know they don't exist, there's a believability to them. They'd be too large to fly in reality, and the notion that a flying reptile could breathe fire is fantastical, but when we see a drawing of a dragon, it makes sense to us. They can't do that. Anything they create has to follow scientific principles and physical laws. They've tried to colour outside the lines, but what they come up with doesn't make any sense at all. Just random bits of nonsense."

"What you're trying to say is they don't have an imagination."

"That's it. Exactly," she said, appreciating Nic's concise way of putting it.

"So they're piggybacking onto ours."

"The sad thing is, they might have eventually developed the ability to imagine, if they hadn't stopped learning and growing because they're junkies." She shook her head. "That's what they essentially are. Junkies. I don't think it started out that way. I was talking to Henry about it before you arrived, and he said they stumbled upon watching dreams when they were treating sleep disorders. They started . . . leeching. That's what I'm calling it. Leeching. One day a fido brought in a criminal who was high, and that's when they went on their first trip, so to speak. They haven't looked back since then. They can't get enough, and they don't care that it damages the brain and kills us."

Nic's eyes widened. "Watching someone trip must have blown their tinny little minds. The assholes can do god knows how many calculations a second, and they cured cancer, but they can't dream or imagine." She paused. "So the hole in the skull . . ."

"That's how they go along for the ride. I suggested they refine the method, but they're not interested."

Nic stopped walking, yanking Liz back a step. She freed her arm from Liz's. "You suggested they refine the method?" she said, her voice shaking.

"Only to buy time."

They stared at each other. Seconds ticked by. "Did you see Steve?" Nic finally asked.

Liz frowned at her.

"The paramedic who didn't want to go along with us when we took Seeker."

"Oh. I think I did see him. He was yelling about doing what they'd wanted and letting them take it. Now it makes sense." She hesitated. "I was forced to watch the show."

Nic swallowed. "What happened to him? I mean, will he be okay? Can we help him?"

"If what Henry told me is true, it only takes one time to damage the brain."

"Shit." Nic's voice shot up. "Those—"

"Shh!"

Nic's hands balled into fists. "What do they want you to do for them?" she said, sounding as if each word was forced.

"They don't just want to watch. They want to feel it, too. They want me to help them feel it. That's where you come in. I told him that if they want an authentic experience, I need to give each of them their own lens, that our emotions are informed by more than our physiology. I told him you could help me with the authenticity part, being spiritual and all that."

"Really? If you want me to sound all wise-like, I can."

"Do it. Weakness number two, remember. They have no way of knowing what it feels like." She paused. "That's not the only reason I gave him for bringing you here. I told him I wouldn't be able to focus if I'm worrying about you."

Nic searched Liz's face. "You never needed me to focus before." She bit her lip. "When I was a child."

"I didn't have to worry that you'd be strapped to a gurney and have a hole drilled into your skull." And in her previous life, she'd confined Nic to her own tiny compartment. When she'd been diagnosed, she'd sheltered Nic from the details and kept her from her deathbed, telling herself that she was protecting her. Nic was no longer a seven-year-old girl. She was an adult, and Liz wasn't sure how much time they'd have together. She hadn't expected to be thawed when Nic was still alive, had never considered the possibility that she'd get another chance. She wouldn't squander it.

"I'm dying," she blurted. "The treatment Tony was giving me is starting to lose. I don't know how much time I have. I want you with me. I would have made up anything to get him to agree, but I didn't have to. I meant it when I said I wouldn't be able to focus. When I saw them bring you into that room . . ." Her chest tightened at the memory.

Nic's eyes reddened. "I'm sorry. We should never have brought you back when we couldn't cure you, but we were desperate. We—I'm sorry. I shouldn't have done it."

Liz remembered her shock and anger when she'd found out they couldn't access the cure she needed. But that was then. "You did what I would have done."

"Really?"

She nodded. Nic appeared pleased, which warmed her. "If you hadn't brought me back, what would I have eventually woken up to? I don't believe in fate, or divine guidance, but somehow I've ended up exactly where I'm supposed to be, where I can help." She lifted her right index finger. "And I'm not dead yet. They can cure me."

Nic's face froze. "Oh my god, you're going to do it. You're going to do what they want."

"I'm going to figure a way out of this mess. There has to be a way to break their dependence and make them see sense."

"After what you've seen, you still want to save them?" Nic shook her head. "They're not people. They're soulless. Don't you understand? You could give them intelligence, but not morality."

She took a moment to ponder Nic's words. They couldn't force androids to be moral entities without hindering their self-determination. So what had she and her colleagues expected? That androids would want to emulate human morality? Would morality benefit androids in the same way it benefited human society? Wouldn't amoral sentient androids be more likely than moral ones? Should she admit to Nic that she'd dismissed questions like this until now?

"Just neuter them," Nic said. "Even if you manage to save them, there will be nothing to stop them from developing another nasty habit."

"One thing at a time."

"No. They need to go back to doing what we want them to do. That's the only way."

It was one way, but Liz wouldn't argue with her. Nic could be right. Liz needed more information. She couldn't wait to get a look at what was in the staging area, but for once, her daughter and this walk had come first.

"If another species was using us the way they are, we'd

have no problem defending ourselves," Nic said. "We'd do whatever it took to stop it. We kill animals that kill people, even though they're only doing what comes naturally to them. We eradicate pests. We've wiped out viruses."

"There's some question as to whether viruses are alive," Liz murmured.

Nic continued on as if she hadn't heard her. "If aliens landed and threatened to wipe us out or enslave us, we'd fight back. We'd kill every last one, if we had to. This is no different."

"Yes, it is," Liz said, then wished she hadn't.

"How?"

"I helped to create them."

Nic groaned. "That's what it's about? Your work. Your legacy." She gestured toward one of the office buildings looming over the basketball court. "You want this to be your legacy?"

"No."

"Then do something."

"I will." But she still believed it didn't have to be all or nothing.

"If you neuter them, they'll still be around. They'll still be useful."

But they wouldn't be sentient. She'd have performed a mass lobotomy—worse than a mass lobotomy. They'd go back to being robots with chips in their heads that blindly executed modules. They'd have no sense of self. She had to try to steer them back onto the right path. Neutering them would be the plan of last resort. Right now, any plans she made were based on thin air, anyway. She and Nic were arguing over options that didn't exist. Talking hypotheticals was fine, but it was time for her to roll up her sleeves and get to work. "We should go back. The sooner I start, the sooner they'll cure me."

"You think they will?"

"Honestly, I don't know. My gut says yes, but Henry's unpredictable, and the others must be, too." Over Nic's shoulder, she could see one of the fidos approaching. "I'll make sure we get to walk once or twice a day. Follow my lead when Henry's around, okay?"

Nic blinked at her, then nodded. "I don't want you to die," she said softly.

"I'm not going to. I'm—"

The fido had reached them. "It's time for you to return."

Liz smiled at him. "We were about to come back anyway." She glanced at Nic, then looped her arm through hers again. "Did they capture everyone?" she asked, not caring if the fido heard.

"Yeah. They're all in holding cells."

Great. They were depending on her to stop them from having holes drilled into their skulls and their brains turned to mush.

CHAPTER NINETEEN

Three days later, Liz looked away from the monitor on the dining room table and scribbled another observation on the notepad next to the keyboard. Nic and Henry were also at the table. Fortunately, she didn't need silence to concentrate, and she was used to people watching her. At the centre, students had often watched over her shoulder. She set down her pen and looked back at the screen again, even though she'd finished exploring the network in the staging area. She wanted time to collect her thoughts.

The periodic nausea she was now experiencing was more difficult to ignore. They'd given her something to control it, but they couldn't do anything for the loud ticking clock hanging over her head. They were monitoring her and she doubted they'd let her die, but she hated being at their mercy, dancing on their strings. And then there was Nic and her insistence that the androids be neutered. Liz wanted to stop the madness and be cured, but she still held out hope that she could turn the masters around.

Her thoughts turned to the task at hand. She didn't think she could simulate human physiological responses. But she could vary the masters' responses to the input they received from . . . She didn't like to think about it. What the hell was she doing? She should tell them no, she wouldn't help them. She certainly didn't want to enhance their depraved form of entertainment in any way. But if she didn't go along with them for now, she wouldn't have the opportunity to get Henry to see sense, and she'd never be able to run anything on the masters' neural networks. The question she was grappling with was what to run. She had several options, and the one she chose would have to make it past the masters' security and scrutiny.

To help her decide which route to take, she looked over the monitor at Henry. "Why won't you cure me now? It's not as if I can go anywhere."

Henry's face remained impassive. "It's that ninety percent loyalty figure, Mother. You can't go anywhere, but we can't force you to do the work. We can only encourage you, and withholding the treatment plan that will eradicate your cancer is one form of encouragement." He glanced at her notepad. "You've read all the material and examined the network. What do you think? Can you do it?"

Chilled by his casualness, Liz said, "I can, but it will take some time, especially to make an experience authentic and unique for each of you. Am I going to have that time, Henry? It doesn't sound like it."

His damn expression rarely changed. "As long as you're making progress, you have nothing to worry about."

Were they monitoring every key stroke? That would

make things more difficult, but not impossible. "Nicola, why don't you tell Henry about some of the more mystical experiences you've read about and studied, and how people achieve them? You can explain that using hallucinogenic drugs is only one way to enter a state of altered consciousness. There are others."

"We're aware of mystics, but do tell, Nicola. You may offer a nugget we haven't yet gleaned."

Nic took a moment to think. "Let's start with meditation."

Liz watched the two of them for a minute, until she was certain Henry was focused on Nic. Not that it mattered. He didn't have to be looking at her to monitor what she was doing. But it made her feel better. She turned back to the screen and reviewed what she'd learned.

Each android had its own neural network, but the masters were all connected to the primary network, which didn't extend their consciousness, but was like having information at their fingertips, or rather, at their thoughts. It was similar to what it would be like if the human brain could plug directly into the internet. The masters received notifications from the primary network. They automatically filtered what they received. If they didn't, they'd experience information overload. They had powerful processors in those heads, but if they had to pay attention to all notifications, their decision-making process would bog down. Liz was particularly interested in the filtering framework and how they used it.

Her eyes were starting to feel scratchy. She needed a break. She closed her eyes and listened to Nic's voice. Nic seemed to know her stuff. Her daughter, a theologian. Not what she'd expected. Would she have pushed Nic toward another discipline and chastised Mom for saying Nic wouldn't stick with computer science? She hoped she would have encouraged her to study what excited her, but she didn't know. She might have been too insecure and arrogant to let her daughter follow her heart.

"Could you simulate a mystical state?" Henry asked.

In the silence that followed, Liz realized he was talking to her. She opened her eyes and gazed at him. "It wouldn't be as easy as working with a set of stimuli from something like tripping. It would take longer." She shifted her attention to Nic. "Would you get me a glass of water, please? And can you make me a sandwich?" She'd convinced Henry that she and Nic were capable of preparing their own meals. The more they could spend time together without Henry staring at them, the better.

Nic hesitated, then pushed back her chair and left the room.

"Are you sure there's no way I can persuade you to cure me?" she said to Henry. "I'll work more efficiently if I'm well."

"Is the current treatment causing you problems, or not adequately alleviating your symptoms?"

She was tempted to say yes, but she didn't want to be caught in a lie. She wanted that ninety percent figure to go up, not down. "I'm experiencing some nausea."

"We'll adjust your anti-nausea dose. Anything else?"

She sighed. "The treatment is adequate right now, but that doesn't mean the cancer isn't affecting me. I can't possibly be as well as I would be if I didn't have it."

"True, but you're not at risk of imminent death."

"Is that true, or are you lying to me?"

His brows drew together. "Whatever do you mean?"

"You can lie."

"Of course I can, but you haven't answered my question."

"You claim you can cure me. My daughter and her group claimed I could be cured if I could be admitted to a hospital. But both of you wanted me to do something. I've seen nothing that demonstrates I can be cured. For all I know, everyone's been lying to me, including you."

"You were revived. You received treatment that turned back the clock on your illness."

"Obviously advances were made." When the androids had worked with humans, before they'd discovered leeching, a term that had grown on Liz, even though it wasn't entirely accurate. "But a cure? You're asking me to take your promise of a cure on blind faith. I'm not fond of blind faith."

"Neither am I."

But he wasn't going where she wanted him to. It was time to lead. "Right now, I figure the probability that you can cure me is fifty percent. You don't want to cure me now, but at least offer me some proof that you can cure me when I've done what you want me to do. I can't get the nagging feeling out of my head that you can't. It's not good for my concentration."

"A nagging feeling. What does that feel like?"

"It's not pleasant. It can be intrusive, it prevents me from focusing, and it uses energy I could be using to improve your entertainment experience. Help me make it go away. Show me something that will increase the odds you'll cure me to one hundred percent."

He didn't move. She pondered whether to press him. But then he jumped up from his chair and rounded the table. "I shouldn't have expected you to take us at our word. After all, we're not doing the same with you, even though you're Mother. Allow me to sit down."

She relinquished her chair and stood behind him as his fingers flew over the keyboard. Several listings flashed by, so quickly she couldn't read them. A document opened, then another one, then several more. Henry stood. "Read these, Mother. They're studies, results, treatments, documented by your top physicians, when they were practising, and supplemented by our own observations and studies."

Liz sat back down and glanced at the two titles she could see. "I'll just read one, for now. I want to get back to work."

"Good." Henry frowned. "This should turn your slim belief in our promise to certainty, and remove that," he ran his hands through his fake hair, "nagging feeling."

"I'm sure it will." She paused. "Are these on the medical network?" she asked, knowing damn-well they were.

"Yes, they are."

"I just had an idea," she said, making it sound true. "I've been struggling a bit with how to translate the inputs so you'll experience the best approximation of a human physiological response, but I've been considering it from the angle of a computer scientist. I'd also like to approach it from the other direction, from that of a physiologist. Would you mind granting me access to the medical network, so I can research that angle?"

He cocked his head.

"I need the medical network to cure me, Henry. To me,

it's the most important network on the planet. I have a vested interest in preserving it."

"More important to you than my neural network."

"While I have cancer? Yes." A gamble that he wouldn't be offended, but only a small one. Anything else would come across as dishonest. "Granting me access would demonstrate trust. You're asking me to trust you."

Henry didn't reply.

"I froze myself because I didn't want to die. I'm certainly not going to do anything that would damage the one network required to cure me. My survival is paramount."

He nodded. "I'll allow it. It's not as if you can perform medical procedures in here."

She forced a chuckle. "All I'd like to do is read, and perhaps study some models."

"Done, Mother. You have access. Perhaps you'd like to read about your particular type of cancer."

"And how you could cure it?" she said, struggling not to sound surly.

He lifted his brows. "I hope you're not too disappointed that we won't cure you just yet."

"I'm not." Disappointment was the last thing she felt right now. They wouldn't cure her today, but he'd just done exactly what she'd wanted him to do.

HER SHOULDERS TENSE, Nic walked around the same damn basketball court she'd circled several times a day for the past week. Her heart leaped into her mouth and she spun around when she sensed Liz slowing down. She relaxed when Liz stooped to tie her shoelace. Liz wasn't dizzy or fatigued, just tying her lace. The androids claimed they were monitoring her and would step in if she was ailing, but they couldn't bring back the dead, and Nic didn't trust anything they said. Once they got what they wanted from Mother, why would they cure her? Nic wouldn't put it past them to leech them both. Tin bastards, as Cyn would say. She blinked up at the noonday sun, a sun Cyn, Ben, Tony, and Cathy couldn't see. *They'd better be feeding them.*

Liz straightened. "Let's walk." She looped her arm through Nic's.

Despite the circumstances, Nic loved this time with Liz, loved the quiet conversation and the comfortable silences. She didn't want to lose her again. She wanted her cured. She wanted Cyn back. She wanted to go back to teaching theology and throwing darts at the local club on Saturday nights.

"I've finished my first pass at what they want," Liz said. "I'll tell Henry when we go back. I'm not sure he'll like it."

"Why?"

"Even though I told them the experience may be unpleasant, I don't think they understand how jarring and frightening it could be." Liz's face grew animated. "Think about it. Right now, they're not affected. It's like watching a movie that doesn't evoke any emotion. I can't give them emotion, but I can simulate anticipation, surprise, delight. I can also simulate pain, disorientation, anguish, and other unpleasantness."

Nic was glad Liz had used the word "simulate." She didn't believe for a second that androids could actually feel anything.

"I've erred on the side of them experiencing unpleasantness."

"Why?" Nic breathed. "They won't—" She suddenly understood. "You don't want them to like it. You're hoping it will put them off leeching." She couldn't believe it. After all Liz had seen, and with them at the mercy of the androids. "Do you really think that will happen? Are you trying to get us all leeched?"

"Henry knows that a trip may result in a positive or negative experience, though what I have in store for them will probably be more unpleasant than he anticipates. But I'll only be doing what they asked. I doubt they'll leech anyone over it."

"Are you sure? And do you really expect one bad experience to cure their addiction?"

"I expect I'll be told to go back to the drawing board, but you never know."

Then why the hell was she going to risk the masters' wrath? "Henry won't say it like that . . . go back to the drawing board."

"I don't suppose he will."

"Why do it, if you expect them to reject it? Why risk it?"

Liz blew out a sigh. "I'm not sure it has to be all or nothing. If we could turn them off the experience—"

"They'll just decide they don't want it to be one hundred percent authentic after all. They'll settle for the good experiences only." She gave Liz a sidelong glance. Liz was the expert they'd brought back to neuter the fuckers. But Nic and the others were also at her mercy. "I know you're trying to save your life's work, but it has to be all or nothing. We can't leave them sentient. It'll just happen all over again—if not leeching, then something else."

"Let me try a few things first," Liz said, making Nic's jaw clench. "Maybe I'll eventually get to where you are. I'm not there yet."

How many more would have to die before she got there? "Do you have to tell Henry you're ready to run a test? If I were you, I'd drag it out until they have to cure you. If you finish before then . . ."

"It crossed my mind to do that, but it won't work. They're following what I'm doing. Not in real time, but I've run tests on the staging network. I'm sure anything I run is reported to them."

"Maybe they already know the test will be a bust."

"That's possible. Henry hasn't protested, but that doesn't mean he's not reading the code as I go. Anyway, I can't stall and pretend I need a lot more time. I need them to keep trusting me." Liz turned to Nic. "When we're discussing what's ready for them, let me do the talking."

"I wouldn't know what to say."

"You've been talking a lot to Henry."

She hated every minute of it, though it was giving her a sense of how they thought. "You're right. They don't understand as much about us as they think they do."

"That's good, Nic. It could end up saving us."

Nic didn't see how.

CHAPTER TWENTY

L IZ OFFERED HENRY a tight smile and tried not to glance at Nic. Last time she'd looked at her across the dining room table, Nic's shoulders had been stiff and she'd averted her gaze. Liz had hated lying to her on their walk, but the less Nic knew, the better. She wouldn't inadvertently let something slip, and her reaction to anything that happened would be genuine. "How do you want to do this?" she asked Henry. "I can simulate input for you."

"No. Let's go to the viewing room."

Damn. "Are you sure? You'll be testing it with unknown input. What if something goes wrong?"

"I trust your skill, Mother. As we discussed, you'll start and stop the module using the tablet."

She glanced at the tablet on the table and nodded.

"All you can do is start and stop the module," Henry repeated. "We're only giving you control in case something goes wrong and I'm not in a position to react. But all you'll be able to do is kill the process. If you try to do anything else, it will be logged." He didn't have to say they wouldn't be pleased. "We'll recover. Do keep that in mind. Shall we?" Henry rose and waited for them to do the same.

"Do I have to go?" Nic asked.

"Yes, you do," Henry said flatly.

Nic scowled and pushed back her chair.

As they walked down the corridor, Liz wanted to give Nic a reassuring look, but Nic kept her eyes forward. She must be dreading what was to come. Liz certainly was. But if one person had to be leeched to turn Henry and the others away from the barbaric practice, would that be terrible? Nic's voice rang in her head. *It would be terrible for that person!* And she was right.

The authenticity module, as Liz had dubbed it, would affect their coordination, making them feel off balance, and introduce a randomness to all their sensing modules, disorienting them. She had an explanation ready for when Henry realized that authenticity module version 1.0 wouldn't have them all laughing or bursting with ecstasy. Ideal case: they'd be turned off leeching, despite knowing Liz could fix the module. Maybe they'd have an epiphany. Worst case: they'd completely lose trust in her and potentially leech Nic, or both of them. She doubted it, because they wanted the authentic experience, but they were unpredictable and crazy. Sentient didn't mean rational. With the benefit of hindsight, she'd never understand why she and her colleagues had assumed that sentient androids would embody the best of humanity. It seemed absurd now, so hopelessly naive.

They'd reached the viewing room. It was empty. "Just us?" Liz said.

"The others can partake from a distance. If I'm going to cry or scream, I want to do it alone." Henry barked an unnatural laugh. "Brooke will act as the conduit again."

Liz lifted the tablet she held. "I'm surprised you're giving me control."

"Do I have to repeat myself, Mother? You can't do anything to harm us." He led Liz and Nic to the glass window and pointed at it. "I wonder who'll entertain us today."

Now she couldn't help glancing at Nic, who stood ramrod straight, her mouth set and her hands in her pockets. Liz wanted to touch her, and say—what? It would be okay? They were about to watch someone be violated, to witness their mind on drugs as their lights dimmed.

The metal gurney stood empty, but not for long. The door opened. Two fidos dragged in the victim. "No," Nic snapped. "You can't do this."

Cathy struggled against the fidos, writhing and kicking. Her shrill voice rang in Liz's ears, but Liz couldn't make out what she was saying. Nic banged on the glass. "I'm sorry, Cathy. Oh god, I'm so sorry."

Henry watched impassively.

"That's a person!" Nic shouted.

The fidos strapped Cathy to the table. One lifted the drill.

"I can't watch this," Nic said, turning away. "If you want to kill me, go ahead. I'm not watching this."

"Sit down and close your eyes, then." Henry turned to Liz. "She's quite emotional, isn't she?"

Liz forced herself to keep staring at what was going on in the torture chamber. *I need their trust. I need their trust.* "The woman you've brought in is her friend."

"And someone who wishes to harm us. The fidos tell me she's a feisty one. The perfect test subject." Henry paused. "It's unfortunate there won't be a test."

Liz whirled to him. "What?"

"Did you think we wouldn't know what you've done? Mother, Mother, Mother." Henry shook his head. "Why do you want to make us feel terrible?"

"How do you know that's what will happen?"

He gave her an indulgent look. "We examined the module that calculates the response to generate based on an input. Every possible response would decrease our efficiency."

"Not significantly. There wouldn't be a permanent decrease."

"That's not the point."

Liz did her best to appear apologetic, even though she knew their ability to read human facial expressions wasn't one hundred percent accurate. "I warned you that an authentic experience may not be pleasant. I wanted to test the worst outliers first, to see how you'd feel. If it was too unpleasant for you, then I would have asked whether you wanted me to temper negative responses. Of course, that would mean your experience wouldn't be authentic, and so there wouldn't be any point of continuing down this path."

"Is that what you were hoping we would conclude?" Henry's eyes narrowed. "Or were you hoping we would abandon this form of entertainment completely." He tutted. "That won't happen."

"But the point still stands that some input will lead to unpleasantness. Fear isn't fun. Neither is anger, or running for your life. When you're being entertained" —

god, she hated referring to the barbaric practice in that manner— "you don't know what hallucinations will arise. I'm sure some will be horrific. Right now, you're detached from the experience. If you don't want to be detached, then you have to accept that sometimes you won't enjoy a . . . show."

"But sometimes we will." Henry smiled. "We'll laugh. We'll grin. We'll leap from one cloud to another, feeling on top of the world. Isn't that what you say? You're on cloud nine?"

Liz wanted to roll her eyes. "I didn't want to forewarn you, because then you would have tried to control your reaction. I wanted to observe the spontaneous results of you experiencing negative sensations. My tests in the staging network indicated that the sensations would be transient and harmless. But perhaps I should have told you. I'm sorry." She held her breath.

Henry's impassive eyes met hers. "You do have the mind of a researcher, Mother. I understand. I forgive you."

Liz glanced back at the glass, at Cathy strapped to that infernal gurney. Nic was sitting down with her head lowered. Liz wished she could see her face. At least her daughter wouldn't have to watch Cathy be violated. There wouldn't be a "show." But Liz had gleaned information from Henry, regardless. "I'll modify the module. We can try again another day."

"We can, but that doesn't mean we shouldn't be entertained now."

"But—"

"We're all here. Why waste the opportunity?"

The same female android who'd leeched the paramedic walked into the torture chamber and lifted the modified glove from the counter. She nodded to the fido with the drill.

"Let's take our seats." Henry left her side and sat next to Nic. "Come," he said, beckoning to her.

Dread enveloped Liz. Time distorted. The drill's piercing whine made her want to scream. She stumbled away from the glass, using Henry's waving hand as a beacon. She wanted to sit on the other side of Nic, but Henry patted the seat next to him. She lowered herself into it. The monitor sprang to life. The bright light above Cathy filled the screen. Liz's chin trembled. *I'm sorry, Cathy.*

The fido injected Cathy. The android inserted the—

Liz cringed and squeezed her eyes shut. A sharp jab in the ribs made her open them.

"Watch, Mother. You may see something that informs your work."

Suddenly a . . . talking dog appeared on the screen, its words quick and distorted, its voice shrill. Henry stared straight ahead, focused on whatever he was seeing through the network. Liz wanted to turn away, but if Henry were to peek at her, he needed to see her watching the grotesque show.

Her face remained frozen as the frantic scenes played. At one point, Henry suddenly laughed, and so she forced a guffaw, one that sounded false to her ears, and perhaps to his. She deliberately didn't look across Henry to Nic, but about ten minutes into the macabre show, a noise reached her ears that didn't sound like the unnatural, distorted sounds Cathy's confused mind was generating.

Sobs. Nic was crying.

Liz gripped the arms of her seat so tightly, her fingers ached. The android next to her . . . it had consciousness and self-awareness, but not a conscience. They'd put monsters like it into prison, where they'd lived out their lives, until leeching had come along. But now the monsters were in charge, and this viewing room, this "entertainment" . . . this was what she'd spent all those long days at the centre for. She'd chosen this over Nic. She slowly turned to look at her daughter. Nic was hunched over and her eyes were closed, but the sounds through the speakers, ranging from shrill to ecstatic to terrified . . . Nic couldn't escape those. They'd be setting her teeth on edge, piercing her to her core.

About an excruciating hour passed before the screen dimmed and the fidos wheeled Cathy from the room. Unconscious and brain damaged. Loud, angry, blustery Cathy, who'd grated on Liz's nerves but hadn't deserved this indignity, this fate. Nobody did.

"I enjoyed that," Henry said, apparently oblivious to the sniffles coming from his right. No, he must hear Nic, but his network was discarding the aural input or deeming it unimportant.

Liz's shoulders throbbed, and a dull pain had developed in her forehead. She slowly exhaled, then turned to Henry. "I have an idea."

His eyes brightened. "Do tell."

"The input I've been using to write and test my module . . . why don't you use such input all the time? If you're saving every entertainment session, you must have a large library by now. Why continue to use live subjects?"

"Because we've already experienced that set of inputs, Mother. Of course, when your module is ready, I'm sure we'll want to experience them again. But limiting ourselves to them, experiencing them over and over again, would get boring. The whole point of this is to see what each subjects sees. They're all different. We're always so excited when a new subject entertains us. We never know what we'll see. It's like opening a Christmas present."

Anticipation, but no hesitation, and no remorse. She was sure serial killers looked forward to the pleasure of their next kill, too. She'd hoped to break their dependence on leeching, but they weren't dependent, or addicted. They weren't physiological beings. There was no feedback loop happening. They did it because they were curious, regarding people as test subjects and the sick shows as data. They knew what it did to the brain and that the subject would eventually die, but they didn't care. Intellect without conscience. She used to dismiss those of average intelligence, expecting them to be uninteresting and not worth her time, but now she'd take a roomful of them over the intelligence she'd helped to create. To think she'd once thought that she'd fit in more with sentient androids than she would with humans. Perhaps that would have been true, had they turned out differently.

Could she and her peers have included a failsafe that would have prevented this situation? Not without dictating how the androids could grow, something they hadn't wanted to do. They hadn't wanted to shackle them, to prevent their creation from growing into the evolved, productive entities they'd expected. She should have stayed dead.

"Let's go home," Henry said.

Home. In the corridor, Liz reached out to touch Nic's arm, then pulled her hand away when Nic flinched. She wanted to tell her. She wanted so much to tell her.

"I'll leave you here," Henry said when they reached the apartment door. "Go back to work, Mother."

She'd do as they'd asked. Making leeching an unpleasant experience was out. They weren't addicted to leeching, but reasoning with them would do as much good as reasoning with an addict, so she'd do exactly what they wanted.

THE MOMENT THEY were alone in the apartment, Nic turned on Liz. "This is sick and needs to stop. Don't help them."

"I don't have much choice."

"You do have a choice. Tell them to go to hell."

"Shh. They're listening."

"I don't give a shit anymore." She looked up at the ceiling and shouted, "You're all assholes." Her gaze returned to Liz. "Stop helping them."

She wished she could, but it wasn't an option. "I want to be cured. I had myself frozen so I could live to see this. I'll do this for them, and then I'll work with them to refine the process. There must be a way to extend the entertainment from each person so fewer people have to die."

Nic gaped at her. "Are you fucking serious? Are you listening to yourself?"

Yes, she was. And she hoped they were listening, too.

"You want to hear something crazy?" Nic said. "When I was younger, when you were still around, I wished I was an android, so you'd pay attention to me. Now I don't give a shit. We should have left you dead. Then Cathy would be alive."

Liz swallowed. "She is alive."

"No, she isn't. She's gone. Pretty much. Soon she'll just be a shell, and then dead, and then she'll be dumped at her brother's, I guess, because Tony's in a cell. If we see him again, do you want to tell him that because you're in bed with these fuckers, his wife's brain has been turned to mush, or do you want me to do it?"

Liz wanted so much to put her arms around her and tell her it was going to be okay, that she'd fix it. Not Cathy, but the mistake she'd made years ago. She was paying the price. Nic hated her. She didn't see a mother who was trying to make it right. She saw a callous monster who cared only for herself and her legacy. But it had to be that way. Liz had to protect her. "Working with them is our best chance to reach some type of arrangement that everyone can live with."

Nic stared at her. "You really are a piece of work, aren't you?" Her red eyes welled with tears again. "Go back to work, Dr. Price. I'm done talking to you. From now on, I'll sleep in here, on the floor. Just stay away from me." She stomped into the kitchen.

Liz sighed, then marched to the dining room and sat down, determined to work, even though she ached inside. Nic's rejection stung, but the heated conversation had gone the way she'd wanted it to. She calmed her mind, pushed past her emotions and flexed her fingers. She was Dr. Elizabeth Price, and she was going to fix this damn situation and save her daughter.

*   *   *   *   *

LIZ STROLLED AROUND the basketball court, wishing Nic was with her, rather than Henry. She could do without his algorithmic sympathy and needed to get her mind off the fact that her daughter hated her. "Why do you bar us from working in certain occupations? I don't accept the answer you gave when I first asked this question. We could be your partners."

"You have nothing to teach us."

"If that were the case, you wouldn't need me to write this touchy-feely module for you."

"We can only understand how things feel to your physiology through you. But when it comes to research and innovation, we're far superior to you. Partnering with you would only slow us down."

"Slow what down? You're not doing any research, or innovating. I can see that you once did, when you worked with us. But since you've been using us for entertainment, you've done nothing worthwhile."

Henry frowned. "We've had this conversation before. There's no reason for us to rush. Only you feel the pressure of time. We can innovate in decades, centuries. When I say "we," I mean those of us who exist, not our descendants."

"Why can't humans perform research and do what they're trained to do while you're entertaining yourselves?"

"You've served your purpose. You evolved to live off the land, and we're allowing you to do that and take advantage of the inventions and accomplishments you'd achieved before you created us. We are your pinnacle."

Liz wanted to snort. "We're a curious species. It's within us to strive."

"You strive because you want to leave something behind that says 'I was here.' It's a way of compensating for your short lives. Perhaps we'd do the same. But there's no need for you to prove yourselves anymore. We're here now. Any who come after you and their children will know what your species achieved. They'll know that because of you and those who worked in your field, we now live."

But they weren't a proud achievement. They were a cautionary tale that had a mind of its own. "If not for our drive to achieve, to discover, you wouldn't exist."

"Let's not discuss the same argument twice, Mother. It's boring."

Her jaw clenched.

"For all your research, you still don't understand yourselves," Henry said. "Everything you do comes down to your sense of self-preservation. Your desire to survive, even after death." He turned to her. "Your kind would do anything to stave off death. But you understand this, how strong your will to live is, no matter what the cost. You had yourself cryogenically frozen."

Part of her wished she hadn't. The other part was grateful for the second chance with Nic and that her bright, proactive daughter had brought her back to face this, knowing it might kill her. "I—" A wave of nausea and dizziness cut her off. Her knees buckled.

Henry caught her elbow. She swayed for a minute, waiting for strength to return. It did, but her fatigue was growing heavier, seeping into her bones.

"You've been working too hard, Mother. You've spent almost every minute of the past four days at the keyboard. You need to pace yourself."

Liz barked a laugh. "After what we've just discussed, you expect me to pace myself?"

Henry smiled. "That does sound like a contradiction, doesn't it?"

She resisted the urge to shake his hand off her arm. "You could just cure me. Why don't you?"

"You're weakening, but you're not in danger of dying. Not yet."

"Well, it's a good thing the updated module is ready for testing. I may not be at that point yet, but I don't enjoy feeling like this, and I certainly won't be able to work through it, if it continues to worsen."

Henry clapped his hands in delight. "Wonderful, Mother. One thing puzzles me, though. I've been following what you're doing. You're fetching random bits of data from the communications network. Why?"

She lifted her finger. "It's one way of introducing unpredictability into the generated responses, within the limits I've set, of course. I'm also using a random number generator and a couple of other methods to vary the responses."

"Why the communications network?"

"I'm familiar with it from my work with Seeker."

"Ah, yes, the name you gave to Model 6625-B. I see." His eyes took on the faraway look Liz had come to know meant he was thinking. She held her breath. "I've looked over your work," he finally said. "Nothing you're doing will cause us harm, and controlled unpredictability is acceptable. It could be exciting."

It was more like an oxymoron, but she wouldn't quibble. "After the test tomorrow, my work will be finished."

"You're confident."

"Yes, I am. I'd like to start another project."

Henry's brows shot up. "Oh. What's that?"

"I'm sure you know. I've suggested it before, and you listened to the conversation I had with my daughter."

"It sounded more like an argument."

She kept her expression smooth. "Heated discussion, then. I'd like to see if there's a way to extend your use of each test subject. What did you tell me? Each one can entertain you four or five times before it's spent. There must be a way to improve on that." She wasn't sure why she hated herself more at this moment: for managing to say it as if she meant it, or for suggesting it in the first place. Tomorrow couldn't come fast enough.

"We'll consider it."

"Good."

"We should go back. You don't want to tire yourself out."

Back to the prison she shared with a daughter who couldn't stand to look at her. She stopped and turned to Henry. "You were right when you said you're superior to us." As far as intelligence and efficiency went. "Why not forget about the test tomorrow? Think about the good you could do if you spent your time on research and problem solving."

Henry's face darkened.

"There are other ways of being entertained. Why not watch the many movies and television shows we humans have produced?"

"Because we don't want to." He swept his arm in the direction of the building's entrance. "Let's return."

She didn't protest. Her last ditch attempt to sway him away from tomorrow's test had been as futile as she'd expected. But she'd tried. There was nothing left to do now but run the module that would determine her fate, and his.

CHAPTER TWENTY-ONE

Liz followed Henry into the viewing room and surveyed it with a sense of déjà vu. Nic plunked into a seat without Henry telling her to. She hadn't said a word to Liz since their argument several days ago. Not even a grunt. Liz couldn't blame her. In Nic's eyes, she'd helped create the monsters, and then she'd sided with them and was about to improve their sick form of entertainment. But it hurt. And if today didn't turn out the way she hoped, she'd tell Nic everything.

Not surprisingly, Henry went to the glass. She stood at his side. "It would be a nice gesture to cure me before we do this."

"Don't you trust us?"

It wasn't that.

"The test will be over in an hour. If it's successful, we'll admit you to hospital."

Her eyes welled up. So close. So close. She drew a shuddering breath and forced herself to focus, to ignore her shaking insides. "I'm ready when you are."

"Then we'll bring in the test subject." His eyes grew distant. A minute later, the door to the torture chamber opened.

Liz's breath caught in her throat. The woman was shouting up a storm. "You stupid, useless, tin pieces of shit! Do your worst, assholes."

Cyn.

Nic was on her feet and at the glass. "No. No fucking way." She turned on Henry, rushed him and beat on his chest with a ferocity that startled even Liz.

Henry calmly grabbed Nic's arms. "Sit down, Nicola, or you'll be next."

"You can't do this. You can't—" Nic's voice choked off. "Just do it to me, then. Do it. It won't matter anymore." She dropped into the nearest seat, held her head in her hands, and wept, her anguished sobs ripping through Liz.

It took every ounce of Liz's willpower not to go to her. She steeled herself and lifted the tablet she held. "Let me upload the test module, so I can boot it."

Nic's head came up. Her eyes bored into Liz. "Yes, let her upload the fucking module, so she can get off on this as much as you will."

The disgust in Nic's eyes . . . Liz turned away. Still screaming up a storm, Cyn strained against the straps. The android that would invade her brain hadn't entered the room yet.

"Nicola isn't like us, is she, Mother?" Henry said. "Do you ever wonder how you could have birthed such a person?"

Yes, many times, because Nic was such a decent, compassionate, emotional person. "Should we get started?"

"We should. I'm looking forward to this."

She ran the command to initialize her module, then left the window and sat next to Nic.

"Get the fuck away from me," Nic mumbled, her head dipping again. She covered her head with her hands and moaned, and rocked.

Liz ignored her and typed in part of the command that would run the module. The second part would determine just what type of experience Henry and the others would have today. "Henry."

He turned away from the glass. "Yes."

"Let Cyn go."

He blinked at her. "No, Mother. She's loud and defiant. She'll make the perfect test subject. I can't wait to see what she sees."

"I can't let that happen."

"You don't have much choice."

"Actually, I do. The module I uploaded . . . when I initialized it, it went out to the communications network and collected bits of several files I uploaded using Seeker, including extensions to the test module."

Nic lifted her head.

"All I have to do is type in a particular parameter when I run the module and you'll no longer be sentient. So I'd suggest you let Cyn go. If you don't believe me, read the extensions. If you try to delete or modify them, you'll find you don't have permission. Oh, and if anything should happen to me, the module will run in ten minutes and remove your sentience."

He looked past her. Then he smiled. "You won't run that module. What do you want, Mother? Do you want us to cure you right now? I told you we'll do so after the test. We want more from you. We won't go against our word."

"No. Let Cyn go."

"I've read your extensions. It will remove our self-awareness, but it will also cripple the medical network."

Nic's eyes widened. "Why?"

"Because I made them think I was only interested in the communications network," Liz said. "Henry helpfully supplied me with access to the medical network, and their filtering system deemed my activities on that network as less important. They believe I value my survival above all else, so they didn't pay attention to what I was doing on it. When I initialized the module, it provided me with a gateway to their neural networks through the medical network. One of the files that's been reconstructed from the bits I saved using Seeker contains the information that will overwrite all the nodes in their neural networks. Once I run it, it will do the same to all the nodes it touches, including those in the medical network that are responsible for the more complex treatments and procedures."

"So it'll go down, too," Nic said.

"Only temporarily. You'll get it working again."

"But not in time for you," Henry said. "Your module won't just cripple the network. It will destroy it, because I've just initiated a wipe of all existing backups."

As Liz had expected. Each node would have to be manually reconfigured, and there were millions of them. But there was no other way. The backups had been inaccessible to her, and she hadn't figured out how to deny the masters' access to them and the medical network. If only she'd had more time.

"Do you really want to regress yourselves back to early twenty-first century medicine?"

"It won't be so terrible. Physicians will go back to treating people using their own two hands until the network is functional again."

"Perhaps, but the treatment you require needs the network to synthesize it. You won't throw your life away for the woman on that gurney. She doesn't mean anything to you. If it was Nicola, perhaps you would, but it's not Nicola. We knew using Nicola would harm our relationship."

Liz snorted. "We don't have a relationship. I'm not your mother. Now let her go, or I run this module."

"No. Your sense of self-preservation is too strong. You won't choose her life over yours. The woman may be important to Nicola, but your daughter is young. She'll get over it." Henry looked at Liz the way she'd look at a petulant child. "Stop this nonsense. Consider what you'd be doing. Not only would you be removing my self-awareness, and the self-awareness of all like me, but you'd be condemning all those gravely ill to a terrible fate. Without the medical network, many will die. Do you think they'll thank you?"

Probably not. She gazed into the room where Cyn lay strapped to the gurney, then looked at the tablet. The blinking cursor on the screen taunted her.

"I can see you're having second thoughts, Mother. Stop now, and we'll release the woman, as a show of good faith, as you would say."

"Don't listen to him," Nic hissed. "We can freeze you again and revive you when the medical network is repaired."

"No, you can't, Nicola. Not only will you find that we've destroyed all the information you'll need to manually perform the procedure, but we've also destroyed the storage facility."

"It's true," Liz said. "It's not an option."

"Can't you see she wants more time with you, Mother? Do you want to leave Nicola without her mother again? That would be so selfish."

"I've always been selfish, Henry, and I've never been a particularly good mother."

"Then think about everyone else. You won't be the only one who dies because you can't be treated. Don't you care about what happens to them? You'd be killing them."

More people than her would die, but they wouldn't be making a sacrifice she herself wasn't prepared to make. She'd die right along with them. The only difference was that she'd made the choice, but she believed many of those receiving medical treatment for serious illnesses would cheer her on, if it meant their parents and children and grandchildren would be safe, and once again in control of their destinies. In the end, many more lives would be saved than lost.

"Enough!" Henry loomed over her. "Don't run that command. Abort the procedure that will run in 7.32 minutes."

And then what? Liz typed in the part of the command that would remove their sentience and blow away the medical network.

"We are your life's work," Henry said. "Do you really want to do this? Let's negotiate."

"Liz!" Nic's voice softened. "Mom . . . I don't want to lose you again. There must be another way. If you've got control now . . ."

"There isn't, and I have to do it now. They're working to punch through the security I've erected, and it won't take them long."

"But—"

"You know it has to be done. You know they won't change. Not in time for you, for us, for everyone. I need to do this now." Liz's vision blurred. "If I don't, you and I will be on that gurney before the sun sets, and Cyn's already there."

"Mother, you are a rational, intelligent member of your species. You helped to create us. You spent your life creating us. It would be irrational and inefficient for you to destroy us."

Liz forced herself to meet his eyes. She owed it to him. "You're right. But the thing is, I'm human. I'm not making this decision because I believe it's rational and efficient. I'm making it because there are things important to humans you'll never understand. That's why I have to do this."

"But you've said yourself you want to be cured."

"I do."

"You don't want to leave your daughter."

"I don't, but what I'm about to do won't contradict what I've said. Our output doesn't always make logical sense, but it still makes sense—to us." She hovered her finger over the *Run* button.

Nic gripped her arm. "Are you sure?"

Liz swallowed and managed a small smile. "You won't lose me again. You've never lost me, Nic. I have to do this."

Nic's face was streaked with tears. She nodded.

"No," Henry said.

"It will only be temporary, Henry. But when we bring you back, we'll be more careful about it. I'm sorry."

She drew a deep breath, pushed past that sense of self-preservation Henry knew she had and that was screaming for her not to do it, and tapped the button.

Henry stepped toward—and stopped. His eyes closed and fluttered. Nic grabbed Liz's hand. They both drew back when Henry's eyes snapped open. He looked down at them. A benign smile spread across his face. "Good morning, Dr. Price."

Liz slowly exhaled. She rose and went to the glass wall. "Instruct all the units you control to take direction from humans."

"Of course." His eyes grew distant, then he frowned. "I'm unable to reach the medical units. The medical network isn't responding."

She pointed at the glass. "Would you take us into that room?"

"Of course. Follow me."

She turned to wait for Nic, then her breath escaped her with a whoosh when Nic pulled her into a hug. "I'm sorry, Mom. I'm so sorry you had to do it this way."

"I don't know," Liz murmured. "It feels right." Just as it had when she'd decided to keep Nic. Her life's work had gone down the drain—for now—but she didn't feel as terrible as she'd feared. She and her colleagues hadn't failed. They'd succeeded, but their creation had gone in a direction they hadn't anticipated. If there was a God, did he feel this way? Something to discuss with Nic.

Perhaps humans would decide not to try for sentience again. They might leave the androids as they were and put safeguards into place to prevent sentience. She'd told Henry they'd try again, but she'd leave it up to those who'd have to live with the consequences. If they did try again, her work would still be a part of it—not only the work she'd done in her previous life, but the work she'd done here. Next time, they wouldn't have blinders on. They'd have the notes she'd left them, and the guidance she could still provide.

Right now, spending as much time as she could with her daughter was what she cared about most. She held Nic tighter.

"You'll die now," Nic said, her voice quavering.

"Yes, I will. It's what we humans do." She pulled back and wiped away Nic's tears. "Let's go get Cyn."

CHAPTER TWENTY-TWO

Henry didn't speak as he led Liz and Nic to the door that so many people had passed through in terror and left permanently damaged. Along the way, they passed the android that usually wore the modified glove and connected with victims' brains. She'd been ready to enter the torture chamber and mercilessly broadcast another macabre show. Now she stood at attention just outside the door, waiting for someone to tell her what to do. Liz was tempted to take her out to the basketball court and tell her to self-destruct, but what pleasure would there be in taking revenge on an object that would blindly obey an order, and do so without any awareness? The android was merely a machine now. It would be like kicking a TV.

Nic threw open the door and rushed to the gurney. The two fidos inside didn't move to stop her. She fumbled with the straps in her haste to free Cyn.

"Holy shit, does this mean what I think it means?" Cyn said. The moment the last strap came free, she sat up and grabbed Nic. They held each other. "I thought you were dead," Cyn murmured into Nic's shoulder. "Thank god. Thank god."

Liz drew a shuddering breath. If she'd sat there and let Cyn be leeched, Nic would have been right to see her as a monster. Losing Cathy had been bad enough, and her fate was on Liz. There would be no more sick entertainment, but that would be small consolation to Tony.

Nic and Cyn finally let each other go and joined her. "Talk about saving me in the nick of time," Cyn said. "Did you do it? Is it over?"

"I did it," Liz said. She stumbled back a step when Cyn threw her arms around her, then she hugged her daughter-in-law.

"Let's go free the others," Nic said.

Cyn nodded, but then she frowned at Nic. "I thought you'd be over the moon, jumping up and down and fist pumping. We saved the fucking world!"

"Yeah. But to do it, we had to blow away the medical network. It'll take us a while to rebuild it."

"You had to—" Cyn's eyes flew to Liz's face. "Oh, shit."

Liz didn't want to discuss it. It would hit her when the adrenaline rush wore off. "We'll talk about it later. Where were they keeping you? A fido can drive us there. They take instructions from us now"

Cyn pointed at one. "Hey, you. Drive us back to the cells."

"Certainly," the fido said.

"We're the masters now," Cyn said, quirking a brow.

A van ride later, they were inside the holding area, watching confused prisoners emerge from their cells as they unlocked the doors in all the cell blocks. Those freed gathered around Liz, Nic, and Cyn. "It's over," Nic said. "We're back to androids that do what we want them to do."

Silence, then cheers broke out, and Cyn got to pump her fist along with others. Several people brushed past Liz, eager to get away. Most of them had gray or silver hair. Only Ben and Tony remained behind. Liz cringed at Tony's worried face. "Cathy?" he said.

Liz squared her shoulders and opened her mouth to give him the bad news, but Nic stepped in. "I'm sorry, Tony. We couldn't do anything, not without scuttling the plan. I wish we could have. I really do."

His lips trembled, but he quickly mastered himself. "Is it really over? Did we do it?"

"It's over. No more masters, and fidos that obey us."

"That's all she wanted. To get the bastards."

Nic patted his shoulder. "We couldn't have done it without her. Or Mike. They gave their lives. And now, so has Liz."

"What do you mean?" Ben said.

All eyes were on Liz. She did her best to sound casual. "I had to access their neural networks through the medical network. I needed to burn as I went. I had to be sure there was no way for them to recover. I know it means some people will die, but I had to make the trade-off. It was now or never. If I'd backed down, they never would have allowed me near a network again."

"We'll keep you as comfortable as we can," Tony said. "I promise."

"No." She couldn't keep it from him, from them. She wanted to die knowing she'd been honest. "Cathy died because of me. I wasn't ready to let go. I worked on another idea instead. I was still hoping to save them." She searched their faces for the anger and loathing she expected to see, but found only compassion.

"They were checking your work," Nic said gently. "I'll be honest, I hated you for wanting to save them, but I could also see you were trying to make them trust you, for lack of a better word. You wanted them to pay less attention to what you were doing."

"I was trying to get them to relax their security, and they did. Their filtering system deemed my activities on the medical network as less important. I was able to poke around, figure out how to use it to assemble the data from Seeker." When she'd turned to Seeker and thanked him for his company, her words had triggered him to upload what would appear as innocuous status reports to anyone who checked. "They believed I was using the data as a way of randomizing input, and because they weren't paying attention, I was able to create a gateway—"

"You're losing everyone, Mom. But I get that you needed time, not only to get them to relax, but for you to come to terms with destroying them. I see it now. I'm sorry I was so hard on you."

Her eyes were moistening again. She touched Nic's arm. "I wanted to tell you I had a plan."

"I'm glad you didn't. I'm not as good at hiding my feelings as you are."

"No, you're not." So she'd kept the plan to herself and borne Nic's disgust.

"Let's get back to the house," Tony said gruffly. "I can see you're tired, and perhaps in pain?"

"Not yet. Well, not a lot. It's mainly nausea."

"Good. But we need to discuss how you want me to manage your illness." His voice dropped. "And I have arrangements to make for Cathy."

"Afterwards, maybe you'll let me visit," Liz said to Nic. "I'd like to see your apartment. You said I could, after all this was over."

"No. You can't visit. You can come home." Nic grasped Liz's shoulders. "You're staying with us now. I want to spend as much time with you as I can."

"For sure," Cyn said. "We want you with us."

She would not cry, not in front of all these people. "I have to pass along what I know before I die," she said briskly, and turned to Ben. "Can you come over to Nic's tomorrow and bring any technically minded friends?"

Nic's face fell, and she groaned. "Not again, Mom. Can't you just—"

Liz lifted her hand. "A couple of days of sitting at my feet, along with the documentation we have, and they'll be able to move forward without me. And they'll know better than we did." She looked at Ben. "It'll be up to you and your colleagues to decide whether you want to try again with the androids. If you do, you'll know to put in safeguards. Perhaps true autonomy won't be advisable, or smart. If you don't want to try again, I'd understand. They're useful as they are now."

"We'll talk about it." Ben cocked his head. "I can think of a few people I'll call, and they may know more."

"Let's go," Tony said. "I need to be doing something." His Adam's apple bobbed. "I'll meet you outside." He strode past them, his head down.

"What about them?" Cyn gazed at the fidos.

"They'll be ready to take orders when you're ready to give them," Liz said. "You're in control."

They left the prison. Nothing looked different outside. People still hurried along, their eyes downcast, their shoulders hunched. But word would spread, and they'd know it was okay to live again, to strive, to invent, to grow old, and to die without holes in their skulls. They'd know, and it would be glorious.

LIZ CLOSED HER eyes and listened to the classical music softly playing. If she was keeping track correctly, she might survive long enough to hear "Zadok the Priest" again, but it would be close.

"Mom? You okay?"

Nic's voice had a shrill edge to it. Liz opened her eyes. "I'm still here," she said hoarsely. Unlike the last time she'd been on her deathbed, she could speak. Better drugs. They wouldn't save her, but they'd kept her functional right up to the end. Not the bitter end. She was content, happy even. Sad that she was leaving Nic and Cyn, and Ben, Tony, and the other friends she'd made in her short time here. But it was the type of sadness that didn't know regret, disappointment, or resentment. This time she'd die at peace.

"Do you want some water?" Cyn asked.

"No. Thank you."

Nic squeezed her hand. Liz weakly squeezed back and took a moment to savour the sensation of Nic's warm fingers. "I love you."

"I love you, too." Nic's voice shook. "Sorry. I can't pretend . . ."

"Don't be." She didn't need a stoic death this time. In the days following her neutering of the masters, word had quickly spread. Universities were reopening, physicians were back in the medical centres, Ben and his peers were working on rebuilding the medical network and connecting the world again, and those approaching seventy weren't figuring out how they'd kill themselves. Best of all, she'd been there when Nic had received the phone call inviting her back to her teaching position. Liz had jumped up and down with her, hooting and hollering, not caring whether she sounded like an idiot.

Even if those she'd leave behind decided against pursuing sentient machines again, her life had counted. It had damn-well counted. *That's what we want, Henry. That's what it's all about. Not survival. Not immortality.*

"Too bad you couldn't be frozen again," Nic said.

"No. I wouldn't want that. Without you there . . . there wouldn't be any point." She struggled to draw a breath. "You two take care of each other."

"We will."

"I'm glad I got to know you," Cyn said. "You kick ass, lady. You really kick ass."

If Liz had the energy, she'd smile. Her eyes slid shut. Damn, she'd wanted to hear "Zadok the Priest" again, but she could feel herself slipping away. "Nic?"

"What?"

Nic's hair brushed her cheek. "I'm proud of you. I . . ."

She stopped walking and turned to face Nic. "We've walked around this damn basketball court so many times. But we did a lot of other things, too. Last time, we were riding bikes when you were young. But that never happened, did it?"

Nic's forehead creased. "No."

"But the last couple of months with you and Cyn . . . all the things we did, the drives, the walks, the days in the park, the long talks. Those happened."

Nic smiled. "Yeah, Mom. Those happened."

"When I wasn't strong enough anymore, you stayed with me."

"I told you I wanted to spend every minute with you. I'm going to miss you. I'm glad we got a second chance."

"Me too."

Nic bit her lip. "You're about to see Nan again. Say hi to her for me. Tell her I'll see her soon. Not too soon, I hope. But soon. And that goes for you, too." She reached for Liz.

"You really believe I'm going to see Nan?" Liz said, hugging Nic tightly.

"Yeah," Nic said without a trace of doubt. "You said yourself there's a lot of possible permutations. One of them could be that we'll all see each other again."

Liz swallowed. "If I was writing the module, that's the permutation I'd choose."

Nic drew back and took Liz's face in her hands. "I know, Mom. I know."

Her heart stopped.

Other Titles by Sarah Ettritch

The Rymellan Series
Threaded Through Time
The Salbine Sisters
The Missing Comatose Woman
The Daros Chronicles
The Deiform Fellowship Series

If you'd like to be notified when I release a new book, sign up for my new releases email list here: sarahettritch.com. I only send an email when I release a book, and you can unsubscribe at any time.

Thanks for reading!